T0128372

CRESCENT BAY

R.G. Chur

Order this book online at www.trafford.com
or email orders@trafford.com

Most Trafford titles are also available at major online book retailers.

Printed in the United States of America.

ISBN: 978-1-4669-2982-1 (sc)
ISBN: 978-1-4669-2984-5 (hc)
ISBN: 978-1-4669-2983-8 (e)

Library of Congress Control Number: 2012907279

Trafford rev. 05/31/2012

 www.trafford.com

North America & international
toll-free: 1 888 232 4444 (USA & Canada)
phone: 250 383 6864 ♦ fax: 812 355 4082

CONTENTS

Book titles by R.G. Chur

Rampant River—Civil War novel—Kansas.

* **Patch**—Drugs and Teens.

English/Spanish Crossover Diccionario—15,000 cognates, bilingual skill guaranteed.

* **Penny the Pink Cloud**—Children story, color and draw.

Crescent Bay—Young Adult novel—teen love, art and football.

* Published by Infinity Press. All titles available in eBook.

CHAPTER ONE

Sunset

THE PAINTBRUSH MOVED with effortless control. Smoky blue sky . . . yellow spring blossoms . . . leaves glossy mint green . . . sunshine gold rays. Sea colors, whitecaps, warm emerald currents . . . Strawberry . . . Silly horn! Connie's brush stalled on a pink cloud line. Her thoughts of colors and the complexity of sun and shade stopped. She looked away from her canvas toward the highway and the Volkswagen bug. Beep! Beep! Beep!

"Yahoo! I'm in love." The driver hollered and waved frantically. Beep! Beep! Beep! A second face popped through the open sunroof. "Hel-lo, beautiful."

The radio blared an oldies tune. "Young Love, First Love, True Devotion." Connie blushed at the catcalls. "Sexists bugs," she yelled. Castaway, an orange ball of fur in her paint basket, hissed. Connie smiled. She was fourteen and realized her petite body in a Catalina swimsuit was a boy-magnet.

The Volkswagen bug was passed by two girls riding ten speed bicycles. More hollering and honking. Connie waved at the girls, campers from the state park. Crescent Bay was a small community. She knew everyone, visitor and permanent resident.

The bicycles accelerated, racing along the edge of El Camino Real. The purple bug leaped forward, the engine popped, the tailpipe sputtered smoke, the speed decreased.

Connie splashed blood red blotches on her canvas. For a moment she wondered why the boy in the back seat didn't howl like a cat in heat. She added a touch of violet to the red, carefully blending the colors together. The sunset on her canvas matched the sun bleeding colors on the horizon.

A tree rose at the edge of her canvas; a limb stretched toward the setting sun. The island cut the horizon, sea and sky a complement of colors. The tree tottered at the edge of the cliff. Ragged roots clung to the cliff face, thick fibers like fingers.

Her brush tentatively flicked forward. "Pop! Pop! Pop!" The bug exploded like gunfire. Connie jerked and smeared red paint on a white cloud.

"Nooo . . ." Taking a deep breath, she sighed and carefully dabbed at the mistake with a cloth. "Same story every year, the city crowd invade the beach town. Boys acting like clowns." Connie smiled at the kitten. "Someday you'll understand, Castaway, when the tomcats start chasing after you."

Castaway stretched and purred agreement.

"And, I'll teach you to love art, like me. Do you like my vortex of colors? Intrusion of purple and orange space, harmonizing blue shadows. Geometric and random shape creating depth and motion. In a simple word. Sunset!"

The kitten mewed, pleased by the attention.

She studied the details of the painting. This was her most ambitious project, Crescent Bay pier. The pier jutted straight out to sea like a ruler measuring the tide. Waves swept the ragged rocks clustered on the south point of the bay creating a natural protective barrier for the boats at anchor. Sailboats, cabin cruisers and fishing boats swayed and bobbed on the rolling tide.

A rock platform at the end of the jetty with a warning light marked the north entrance to Crescent Bay. The tide was in, only the top of the jetty was above water. Waves splashed over the rocky path to the stone platform ascending from the ocean like a pyramid with a flattop.

Connie remembered being trapped on the point one afternoon. High tide caused by a full moon flooded the jetty's path with waist deep water. Fortunately, she was with friends. They held hands and managed to wade ashore, pausing when the waves swept the rocks. It was rare for the tide to be high enough to cover the rocks. The tide was never high enough to reach the light platform.

The kitten leaped from the basket and pranced on the black and white striped beach towel.

"Too hot, little friend?" Connie's brow crinkled and she wiped the sweat away. The temperature was nearly ninety; a slight sea breeze cooled her face. Sunset will drop the heat ten degrees. And sunset was happening minute by minute.

A pair of pelicans circled the bay looking for dinner. The leader suddenly dove, plunging headlong into the sea. The head popped up; the beak clutched a fish. The bird tilted the beak up and swallowed. Connie added two birds to her canvas with swift brushstrokes. Flipping the brush around, she used the round point of the handle to engrave detail: eyes, a beak and wing tips.

"Tomorrow I will paint you into the canvas." She waved the brush at Castaway. The kitten flicked a paw at the silvery threads.

Connie compared her painting to the event, the sun half submerged in a velvet sea. The breeze kicked sand around her toes. From her vantage point atop the cliff the bay before her was shaped like a taunt bow with the pier as the arrow bisecting the center of the bow. Not the longbow of Robin Hood legend, but rather the deep bow Cupid used to insure love between unsuspecting couples.

When the wind comes late in the day the people leave the beach. The girls fold aluminum chairs and bookmark romance novels. The boys jog home, darting glances at girls in bikinis. Children with buckets and balls follow moms to the parking lot. Sand castles surrender to the tide. Ambitious to catch all the detail on her small canvas, Connie labored to succeed, dabbing a flash of orange as the sun sinks below the sea. Twilight ended her work.

She folded her portable easel, the canvas still attached, shielded by plastic. The pier she was painting needed more rust color. The old pier, a sentinel guarding Crescent Bay, still standing despite the caustic elements of nature attempting to tear the pier from the shoreline and the efforts by some residents in the resort to replace the relic.

The wind and rain and rushing tide had left scars, but the pilings were reinforced a few years ago. Otherwise, the pier surely would have toppled in last winter's El Nino storms. The pier stands against time, stands against the harsh treatment of storm and tide, defiant. The pilings are home to clusters of seashell, mussel, and starfish. Connie wondered, perhaps some supernatural power was watching over the old structure.

Certain tenants, including her father, considered the pier to be an eyesore marring the crisp features of the new deluxe resort. Connie frowned. She loved to draw and paint the old pier. She felt bad that her dad was part of the vanguard to replace the old pier in the name of progress.

Connie knew the history of Crescent Bay. She had lived at the resort for the past two summer breaks from school, and had camped in the state beach park almost every summer since she was five. The Indians lead the first Spanish Missionary to Crescent Bay. It was a secluded bay, a night camp on the old Spanish trail that meandered over steep hills and through narrow arroyos to the Santa Barbara Mission.

In 1808 the shallow bay was pinpointed on nautical maps of the Southern California coastline. The name Crescent Bay was chosen because of the shape of the bay, like a lazy quarter moon carved between towering cliffs. A large seal population lived on the rocks offshore. Fishing was the early inhabitants main occupation. Gradually, retired people found the bay and the tourist followed.

The locals lived a relaxed lifestyle. Cottages ran along the cliff edge and dotted the hills behind the bay. A collection of business establishments and beach apartments stretched along half the bay-shore. The new resort covert half the north side of the bay. Every summer the tourists doubled the population of Crescent Bay.

Connie tucked her paints and brushes into her belt pack, gripped the handle of the collapsible easel and headed down the path. Castaway mewed and stuck her head out of the basket to check direction. Someday she would walk the path alone, prowl at night. The kitten bounced along, big eyes staring ahead, recording every landmark.

Connie continued to mentally compare her painting to the scenery surrounding her. Colors changed tones and shapes changed proportions as she moved down the path. The cluster of fishing boats moored haphazardly along the stretch of shallow bay grew larger and seemed more in line, pictured from this angle of view. She studied the handful of sailboats and pleasure craft, the colors subdued by absence of sunshine. Three jet skis whipped around the boats and raced at top speed out of the bay. The five mile per hour buoy rocked violently.

"That would be my brother, the reckless fool. Don't you ever listen to him, Castaway. Whenever he's around, you run away and hide." Connie felt the kitten brush against her wrist. She watched the jet skis circle around the rocks. They were heading for the state campground, a narrow stretch of beach south of the bay.

Connie quickened her pace. In the hills above the campgrounds a dozen hot mineral pools attracted health enthusiasts. Connie knew of another mineral pool north of the bay with Indian hieroglyphics etched on the rocky outcroppings around the pool. The rolling hills stretched inland. The snowy peaks of the Sierra Mountains loomed above the hills. Scattered across the landscape were small towns, man-made lakes, vineyards, cotton fields and tree farms.

North of the bay was a collection of homes on a high mound. The structures looked like an abstract collection of blocks colored not to match. The last splash of sunlight flamed on the windowpanes. Stretching toward the faded blue sky, antennas and telephone poles received the latest world crisis and sitcom silliness.

A string of lights blinked alive on the pier and glowed brightly. A cluster of teens stood around the rickety shack at the base of the pier. Seven pilings kept the squat little building from toppling into the sea. The owner, an older man in a wheelchair named Eddy, rented surfboards and sold hotdogs, chips, and sodas.

The purple Volkswagen rumbled down the road and parked on the blacktop parking. Two guys leaped from the front seat and ran toward the food shack tossing a football on the way. Connie watched from her vantage point at the corner of the parking lot. She frowned. "Our friendly hooter, sexist jocks. And, the third too shy to appear. Meet the sunshine tourist, Castaway. Promise not to scratch and bite."

The kitten hissed disapproval.

Connie crossed the parking lot and ignored the two jocks. Connie was equally ignored because their complete attention was on the two girls beside their bikes near the snack shack. The boys raced in that direction.

She studied the boy slouched in the back seat of the bug. Dark eyes stared in her direction. Big sad puppy eyes, she thought and wondered what his problem was.

She took a long look at the artwork painted on the VW door. Sharp perspective lines created a narrow cubical design. Under the gold football trophy were neat geometric letters, KNIGHTS.

"Knights of the square table from the realm of squares." Connie patted the kitten. "What do you think, Castaway?"

Kitten eyes looked up at her expressing total agreement.

Across the parking lot was a gated road to the resort condominiums. A golf course was being built behind the resort, a rolling hills course with cliff edge bunkers and a small salt-water lagoon. Another project of her father and his cohorts for change. She hated to see the landscape blemished with sand traps and cultivated greens. She loved to paint the natural wild beauty of the land.

The football jocks were near the pier. The girls straddled bikes and pushed off. The girls kicked hard and directed the bikes to a path that lead to the state beach camp. The boys gave chase for fifty yards but gave up hope and stopped following.

Connie pressed security buttons, giving the code to open the gate. After sundown the sea and sky turn black, stars flicker. The jetty, a dark strip of rocks falling off the edge of night. Connie hurried up the walkway to her front door. The basket rocked, a sleepy kitten purred.

CHAPTER TWO

Granddad

A SIX-FOOT LENGTH of metal corrugated fence, one end nailed to a corner post, flapped in the wind. A duplicate strip half buried in the sand, stretched like a gangplank to the edge of the cliff. Six more posts surrounded the brick porch; white gull droppings crowned the tops. Ice plants ran wild around the bungalow and over the cliff. Five hundred feet below white surf rippled over golden shore.

The bungalow was a square squat building coated with peeling blue paint. A big window and a door with a porch faced the sea. A pair of rusty motorbikes leaned against the south wall. On the north side was a stone chimney. The path leading to the front door facing the street was brick, stained green from moss.

"Need to stock some firewood, beach driftwood works well. Of course, it being summer you hardly need the heat. Might be best to leave the fireplace without a fire." The older man's monologue continued. At the diner he had greeted his grandsons and their friend, Carlos. He hugged each in a bear grip, showed them the diner and explained their job. He asked about their mother and father, reminisced on family history before and after the recession. He continued to talk and talk and talk. And he changed the subject every five minutes.

"I expected you boys before now." He scratched his white beard, a frequent habit.

"We stopped for hotdogs on the way. Tossed the football around. I'm on the varsity squad." Mark, the oldest grandson explained, forgetting to mention the girls they jogged after. "My friend, Carlos, is a star receiver."

"That's right, you boys play football, college."

"High school," Mark's best friend corrected.

The older man's eyes brightened. "I remember my school days, ran the mile in track, no football. But, I know the game. I've been showing Lloyd, my night cook, a few tips on the game. He plays football at the local college. All American game." Without a pause in words, he unlocked and opened the door to the bungalow. The hinges protested, screeching horribly.

"Once I rented this bungalow and two more like it. I was building a fourth when fire burned down every bungalow except this one. Welding torch accident. That was back when they built the resort; I wanted to keep competitive in the tourist business. But I couldn't afford to rebuild. This last bungalow became storage for the diner." He took a long breath and waved his hand at the collection of kitchenware. Boxes were stacked over halfway to the ceiling along one wall.

"Pick out what you need: glasses, dishes, pots, utensils, whatever. This is all odd stock from the diner. You boys can move the boxes into the railroad car behind the diner. Last year I bought the railroad storage container, better lock-up. Never got around to moving the diner supplies." He twisted the end of his mustache.

"Now, this rental is just a dusty relic. Use to rent to truckers for a night sleep, before the freeway was built east of here. That new freeway diverted traffic off the coast road. Hurt business, but the diner survives and still pays the bills."

Our new home for the summer, Mark thought. A place to train, to practice football everyday, vigorously, to prepare for the season. Ultimate goal, to win the senior year championship. He was lucky his grandpa owned a truck stop diner. Mark and his friend hired on to wash dishes and bus tables for the use of the bungalow by the sea. No free ride from grandpa. The beach just below was the training field. Every free minute they would practice. Paul, his brother, was along for a different reason.

"Door needs oil on the hinges, dusting inside, maybe a little paint. The roof don't leak and you have sleeping bags. Remember, no girls or booze in the shack."

The rising moon was lighting the starry sky. A cool sea breeze whipped his windbreak. Paul wrapped his arms across his chest and shivered. He didn't want to be here, trapped in a sleepy anchovy town. Wiping stinking dishes. And, this dump?

The blurred front light flickered and glowed revealing spider webs crisscrossing the doorway. The only thing he'd seen so far of interest was the girl painting, her jet black hair streaming in the breeze. He thought she was too young for the two stupid football clowns.

He followed his brother into the building. No! He didn't want to be with his brother. He didn't want to be in this dank moldy smelly old room. He wanted to be home with his friends. But, he committed one unpardonable sin, one mistake—tagging. He was caught and he was exiled. Worst than exile, forced servitude, dish-master at his grandfather's diner.

"Let me get this here light, figure the bulb is loose." The switch clicked and clicked and the light flashed twice and lit.

A seashell wind-chime hanging in a broken windowpane, clicked and clacked. "The perfect weather gauge." The old timer chuckled. A fly buzzed through the opening and was trapped in a spider web. I rented to an artist before the recession. She painted the letters on the wall." LOVE in bold letters and bright wild colors covered one wall. "She painted seascapes mostly." He turned and pointed.

The three boys stared at the large painting on the opposite wall. An outlandish display. Homemade burlap canvas weaved together thickly, stapled and glued to the drywall. A huge square seascape with spears of light cast toward the center. The colors outrageous, all wrong, purple waves, yellow sky, orange clouds. A boogie board, tilted in the corner, was painted the same wild colors.

"This is the main room with bunk-beds and couch. Open kitchenette to the left and the bathroom right through that door. Sorry, shower only. A bookshelf with a rare collection of National Geographic. Lounge chair, coffee table." Granddad pointed to each object on his inventory. "Fully furnished. Of course, the avocado crate is rustic. That green porcelain dragon lamp fell off a truck full of furniture."

Dust covered everything. A small portrait of Elvis, tilted, revealed a hole in the plaster wall. Smoke stained the icebox, lampshade, and Venetian blinds. Beside a record player was a stack of cowboy records. A torn curtain hung above the sink blocking half the window. The faucet dripped.

"Expected you boys earlier. I have brooms and a mop, some buckets, and extra-strength cleaner all ready. Didn't promise a rose garden. Needs some cleaning up. Right now it's too dark to work. First thing in the morning, you get the cleaning supplies from Martha, she cooks breakfast and lunch at the diner. I need one of you boys on the dish rack to cover the morning shift." He paused and took a deep breath.

"Arrange your own schedule. Share the day with five hour shifts, or two work eight with a day free, rotate the shifts. Doesn't matter. Morning, noon, and evening someone works the dish rack. The night cook, Lloyd, is Martha's son. Martha has a friend works six to closing, helping to prepare salads, baking, and cleaning-up. You boys decide the work rotation. This is gonna work out fine, boys." The old man flashed white teeth, with glints of metal. His eyes peered from a bony skull, his face a map of wrinkled lines.

"We'll work out a schedule, grandpa," Mark said.

"Be careful cleaning up the bungalow. Watch for black widow spiders. A black spider with a red dot. Seen a number myself. Always be careful."

"We'll check for killer bees too." Mark winked at his friend. "And, rattlers. Can't be too careful."

Paul kicked the sofa and a mouse ran out from under and scampered into the kitchen. Carlos screamed, "Snake!" He leaped on a rattan chair.

Mark laughed. "A mouse, Mr. Macho."

The old man cackled, "Can't be too careful. You boys pack in your sleeping bags and settle in. Something to eat in the diner if you're hungry. You just ask if you need anything. I'll see you boys in the morning. Here is the key. You boys have any questions?"

"No sir, thank you, granddad, we'll be fine." Mark took the key.

"In the morning, then. You boys sleep well. I'll call your mom and tell her your settling in. Good to talk to your mom." The door edged shut and the room was silent for a long moment.

"First, something to eat." Mark suggested.

"I'd say another hour conversation with your grandpa rules out the diner." Carlos opened the icebox. Empty, except for a crusty jar of peanut butter with green mold growing inside.

"We have to eat at the diner soon enough. Good enough for truckers." Mark slapped the back of the sofa. A cloud of dust rose in the air.

"Truckers listen to country western music all day and breathe diesel fumes," Carlos said. His stomach growled.

"I like country western." Mark frowned. "Unlikely pizza is served in the diner. We'll try the pizza parlor we passed down the street, other side of the bay, near that fancy resort."

"Count me out," Paul said. "The hotdog at the pier was my dinner. And, I'm tired."

"We'll bring you back some pizza."

Paul listened to his brother and Carlos laughing while walking to the car. They were probably glad to be rid of him. He obviously wasn't having fun.

He walked out the door and around the bungalow to the cliff edge. The lights of a ship moved slowly across the dark water. He looked straight down at the white combers rushing toward shore.

He stepped closer, clinching his fists, remembering. Tagging the freeway sign, forty feet above traffic on a catwalk. His friends, Victor and Raul, passing him spray cans. The police siren blaring, his friends running. He was scared. He moved too quick, slipped. He rolled over the edge of the catwalk and clung to the narrow ledge with one hand, hanging over the freeway. Paul shivered, felt goose bumps raise on his skin. It was all to real a picture in his mind. Car lights racing at him in the darkness. Horns honking. Fingers clutching cold steel, weakening.

The flashlight in his eyes, blinding. "Hold tight!" The urgent command. The policeman looming above him, reaching.

He remembered the policeman's face in the glow of the headlights, the eyes sincere, determined, life and death in the balance. A man dedicated to help people. The click of metal, his wrist shackled. His fingers numb, released their hold. The cop's wrist was snapped to the other handcuff. Paul was pulled up, driven to the station, and booked.

He remembered the jail cell. A cage, one bunk and a metal toilet. He sat on the bunk in the corner, a frightened, trapped animal. He remembered his father's eyes, old eyes, disappointed and concerned. Released at two in the morning, he was lucky to be alive.

He sat cross-legged on the edge of the cliff. He didn't feel guilty for tagging. But, he felt remorse for hurting his parents, disappointing them. And the punishment? Banishment for the summer. No friends, no fun, no girlfriend. No Betty, his friend's sister, his date to the junior high school prom. They planned to hang-out together all summer long. Restriction! No summer vacation.

Tagging wasn't a big deal. He was just having fun. It was neat to see his arty letters. He was proud of his graffiti. The illegal graffiti. They should have tagged in the riverbed. Tagging the freeway overpass was a bad idea. He felt confused.

Life was confusing. Now, he had to suffer for his poor judgment. Perhaps try to make amends. He didn't mean to hurt his parents or anyone.

The punishment was unfair. His only crime was defacing public property. And, breaking the curfew. Trespassing. Okay, he was a criminal. "Your granddad will watch you," His father warned. "You work and you behave or next stop, military school."

He didn't feel like a criminal. He loved his parents. He did his homework, never ditched. He respected adults. Graffiti art was just his thing. Usually the riverbed was the canvas.

That night his friends decided to exhibit on a freeway overpass. Everyone would see their art. He protested, but he went along.

Paul stared down at the waves shattering against the rocks. He whistled softly. Shrill notes pierced the night. It seemed that each note brought the waves higher and made the flying surf sing louder.

Paul looked up at the stars, his eyes misted with tears.

CHAPTER THREE

Jet Ski

CARLOS KEPT PACE beside his friend, his long strides eating up yardage. A pleased grin spread across his face; he was humming a song. Carlos was deep into music. He studied flute in school and played guitar for fun. He even wrote his own lyrics, mostly romantic.

Mark zigged and zagged; Carlos followed suit. Good, Carlos wasn't dreaming, Mark thought and quickened his pace.

"Pass or run, a quarterback choice? Play 96 or 81. Hup, hup, hike!" Mark tossed the tennis ball laterally to his friend.

"I'm free, downfield, in position." Carlos caught the ball and flipped it back.

"Visualize each play, memorize every move." Mark repeated the coach's instructions.

The two jocks ran along the beach, huffing and puffing, swapping football theory, most of the principles learned from Coach Kramer when they were sophomore rookies. The tennis ball exchange sharpened their ball handling skills. The coach's trick.

The sun was balanced on a hazy horizon. They had finished their stretching leg exercises, knee squats, push-ups, jumping jacks, and short sprints. After the warm-up, an hour of jogging had brought them to the public campground.

"Now shake out the body." The words of their coach, a drillmaster, were parroted by Mark. The two young men gyrated, jumped and jerked, allowing muscles and nerves to go limp. They relaxed, taking a break before the jog back to the bungalow.

The smell of wood smoke wafted in the air. Early risers prepared coffee and breakfast on camp stoves and campfires. The tide was low. An older couple, clamming in rubber waders, jabbed the sand with pitchforks, striking for a clam. A fishing boat trolled outside the surf line. The sun was slowly burning through the morning haze.

A line of seagulls flew over and watched the boys toss the tennis ball back and forth. The boys were determined to pass a football with the certainty of a juggler.

Mark leaped for a high toss and back-peddled into a sand dune. His shadow cast a giant image against the wall of sand. Mark grinned. "Idea! Look, the opponent. Bigger and quicker. Watch me take him down."

Mark charged the flat face of the sand and slammed into his shadow. "I've knocked out our opponent's left tackle."

"I'll take out the right tackle." Carlos dodged and weaved and flattened against his shadow. "Yowl!" He howled.

"What's wrong? Did your shadow bite you?"

Carlos backed away. His arm was scratched and bleeding.

Mark looked at the hole his friend had plowed into the sand. "Razor clam." He plucked the shell from the sand dune.

"Anymore bright ideas?"

Mark smiled. "Girls."

Two girls stepped from a camper. A voice yelled, "Be back by noon to watch your baby brother."

"Yes mom, noon, watch Andy," the tall redhead acknowledged. The girls jogged past the boys to the water's edge. Both girls wore tight T-shirts with the words "Soccer Rules" on the back. The tennis ball bounced off Carlos' head. The girls gingerly stepped into the shallow surf.

Mark touched the cool wet sand. He took a sprinter position. "Surfs up!" He shouted. "Yahoo!" And rushed for the sea.

Carlos hesitated. "Football and exercise, remember. The coach said swimming was excellent exercise for the whole body." He dashed for the sea.

The two boys charged past the girls and dove into the cold surf. They surfaced and turned to smile at the girls.

The girls churned the shallow water, running in place. A warm-up exercise, Mark realized. The pair jogged away. Mark thrashed in the surf. A wave crashed over his head and pulled him underwater.

He surfaced and saw Carlos struggling to reach the shore. His friend never gave-up on a chance to meet girls or win on the football field.

"Hurry," he yelled. "Not a moment to lose. We'll catch-up."

"We're here to train, remember." Mark caught a wave and body surfed toward his friend. Together they panted and trudged up the beach slope, feet sinking deep into wet sand. A sandpiper on long stilt legs poked the sand with a stiletto beak hunting crabs. Chil! Chil! Chil! The bird admonished the intruders.

"Ever hear of mixing business with pleasure," Carlos said.

"Remember, last game of the season, the championship on the line? The score tied and the pass bobbled. The interception that lead to defeat. Remember?"

Carlos remembered. Two tackles caught him in a scissors and crushed the wind out of his chest. We learn from our failures, the coach consoled. And, we always have next year. Practice, practice, practice was his mantra.

"We need to redeem ourselves. And that means hard work and practice. All summer, practice. That's the plan. And, girls are not a part of the plan." Mark took deep gulps of air. The surf pulled at his feet; he plunged out of the surf. "I was wrong."

Carlos grinned and jogged away. "They can be our cheerleaders. Pom-pom girls."

"You're hopeless."

Carlos yelled after the girls, a hearty hello. The thundering surf crushed his words. The surf was above six feet. A storm off the Baja Peninsula fed the wild surf. A cluster of jagged rocks prohibited surfing further south of this stretch of shoreline. But, along the mile front of the campground surfers dotted the curling waves. Carlos ran after the girls. Mark followed.

Thirty minutes later, fallen far behind the girls, whizzing, they stopped.

The old pier was in sight, and the girls were climbing the road toward the diner. The boys stood at the base of the rock jetty protecting Crescent Bay from the open ocean.

"Time for breakfast, mate." Carlos bent over, chest heaving. "Those girls are fast as jackrabbits."

Carlos looked at his wristwatch. "Carlos, we only worked out for an hour and twenty minutes."

"We can't miss breakfast," Carlos grumbled.

"You ate a cinnamon donut and drank a hot chocolate for breakfast. And you downed two slices of left over pizza."

"That is not breakfast. That's not even a snack. Comprehend amigo."

"Your only interest is the girls."

"Not true, I'm starving."

"Another hour and we'll eat."

"Half."

"The purpose is to get fit, not flabby."

"I'm not flabby. And, you need food to burn energy."

"You have plenty of stored fat; you need to slim down."

"We'll pack a lunch, tomorrow." Carlos' stomach growled.

"Breakfast after we conquer the rock jetty."

"The idea is crazy, Mark. Jumping from rock to rock. The idea is dangerous." Carlos stood straight. He looked at the waves crashing over the point of the jetty, spraying the light tower.

"This will work. Trust me. The exercise will make us the best dodge and run players on the team."

Mark ran forward and jumped to the top of a rock. Three hundred yards of tumbled boulders the size of their Volkswagen stretched out to sea. The jetty protected this side of the bay from the heavy southern breakers. On a higher, flat bed of rocks at the end of the jetty was a warning light. Mark zigzagged across three more giant rocks. "A piece of cake. The lane is ten yards wide and the cracks no larger than a foot."

"But the surface is uneven and slippery from the morning fog." Carlos carefully climbed to the top of a rock.

"No, the rocks are dry, safe as a stroll down Christmas Lane." Mark leaped forward.

Carlos stretched his long legs and jumped to the next rock. He firmly planted his feet and surveyed his next move.

"One small leap for football. Take it slow." Mark advised.

"I still think the idea is crazy." Carlos jumped to the next rock, steadied himself and jumped again. "Look, I'm a frog." He laughed and leaped forward.

"Careful. Don't crack a knee or your head on the rocks." Mark stumbled, pitched forward, caught himself. He leaped forward to the next rock.

"You be careful, hotshot." Carlos stretched his arms like a tightrope walker, balancing carefully.

The sea surged through the rocks. Pounding drums rumbled in the hallow chambers. The pair carefully moved forward. Youthful enthusiasm strengthened their confidence and soon they were near the end of the jetty.

The whine of an engine cut across the sound of the rush of white water against the jetty. A jet ski flashed around a cluster of rocks jutting from the sea and roared toward the point of the jetty. Mark watched the ski rider whip past a sailboat forcing the sail to veer radically to port. Power against sail, Mark thought. The sail was lucky to avoid the powerful jet ski. The small sailboat had the right-of-way.

The jet skier expertly jumped the wake of a fishing boat heading out to the kelp beds to fish for albacore. Mark turned and there was Carlos. His big friend lumbered past. "First to the point." He challenged.

Mark grinned and watched his big friend leap ahead. He moved with a grace that big men often exhibited. Mark could catch him, but he waited. Then, he advanced swiftly.

Mark looked again toward the jet ski. He was coming straight toward the jetty, full throttle. He rounded the point, cut parallel to the jetty, and banked his ski. A jet of water hosed the jetty and caught Mark in the face.

The salt stung and blinded him. He pitched forward. His body struggled for equilibrium and failed. He slammed against the rock, his hand caught in a crack, his wrist bent, twisted. His breath came in a ragged gasp. Excruciating pain shot up his arm. He felt faint.

"Hooray! Wipe-out! Yahoo! Wipe-out!" The jet ski whipped around the point of the jetty. The rider was screaming like he won a target shoot.

Mark gingerly eased his hand free. Gently he flexed his fingers. They were unbroken. He rotated his wrist and winched.

Carlos was hunched over him. "That jerk! Are you hurt, Mark?"

"I'm okay. Bruised. My wrist is real sore." Mark cradled his hand and wrist against his chest. "I don't think I broke any bones."

"We'll have you checked out," Carlos said. He grasped Mark's left hand and helped his friend stand.

"Sure, I'm okay. Just shook-up and mad as hell. That ski jerk." His wrist throbbed.

"I've seen you toss the football with your left hand."

"Sure, sure." He grinned

The high-pitched whine of the jet ski echoed across the sunlit sea. Mark extended his left arm and shook his fist. "Someone needs to teach you a lesson." His eyes blinked tears and the jet ski blurred.

CHAPTER FOUR

Frank's Diner

PAUL OPENED THE screen door and stepped into the kitchen of his granddad's diner. He was hungry and the cooking smells made his mouth water. The kitchen was immaculately clean. The stainless countertops were spotless and the cupboards dustless.

Lloyd, the night cook, tilted back on a chair. He was reading a thick book. A big woman prepared food, juggling plates, spatula and spoon. She never stopped moving, a rhythmic dance. She flipped flapjacks off the griddle onto a plate and scooped grits from the steam table. She added eggs over easy, sausage, and parsley garnish. "Order up!"

A pretty waitress, that would make his brother drool, picked up the order. His brother and Carlos were on the beach having fun. The three boys had drawn straws to see who worked the first shift the first day and Paul was the loser. He was sure his brother somehow fixed the drawing.

The woman slapped the grill with the spatula and looked up from her work. Huge black eyes looked into Paul's eyes. Paul felt like she was searching his mind. "You the new boy? Put on that apron. Start to scrub the pots in the sink. I'm Martha and this is my boy, Lloyd. He just stopped for breakfast before going off to class. He works the night shift and attends college in the day."

Her son blew a kiss at his mother and waved at Paul.

"My boys in college studying plants."

"Genetic alteration of plants for space application, mother. Particularly, experimentation in the adaptation of genetically altered micro organisms to create growth on Mars, terraforming." Lloyd flipped the page of his notebook and continued to jot down information from the text.

"My son, the genius."

"I'm happy to meet you both. I'm Paul."

"You get hungry, call out. Usually, you get here early to eat. But, this is your first day. You get a break after the breakfast crowd."

For the next hour Paul made repeated trips to pick up dish trays. Lloyd showed him how to work the dishwasher. He stacked dishes, rinsed and ran the dishes through the dishwasher. He glanced at the clock, time dragged. Martha's critical eye kept watch on him.

Once when he returned a tray to the counter unwashed after dumping napkins, Martha warned him to wash the tray every time it was used. "The health department is watching us," she explained. "Read the sign on the side of the tray." On each tray was the stenciled message: Wash Tray After Every Use.

Paul pushed open the kitchen's swinging door and walked to the bus tray full of dishes under the counter. He smiled at the girls seated at the counter sipping cokes. The job had some perks, he thought. They smiled back, giggled, and continued their conversation. Probably deciding he was too young. Mark and Carlos matched their age. Not that age mattered.

The door of the diner opened and a barefoot youth entered in wet swim shorts and a yachting cap. He was barefoot. Paul remembered the sign he read on the door. No Shoes, No Service. The new customer sauntered over to the girls.

"Hello, beautiful campers, may I join you? And, invite you sailing." He grinned and pointed to the cap. "Captain of a catamaran."

"Arnold, you asked us yesterday, and the day before. Please don't ask us again. You're wasting your time." The blonde girl's voice expressed annoyance.

"Coffee for the captain, swabby." Arnold looked straight at Paul.

Paul hefted a tray of dirty dishes. "You need shoes to be served." He smiled at the girls. "Refill when you're ready."

"Kitchen boy, keep your garbage eyes on the garbage. And, keep your mouth closed." The older boy glared at Paul.

Martha opened the kitchen door. "You want to stir up trouble? This boy is a worker. You call him names. You lack respect." Martha pointed to the door. "Out."

"I was having breakfast with the girls. My treat." Arnold winked.

"Arnold, we're not with you. We pay for our own food. And, the busboy is just doing his job. You try to be adult but act like a child." The girl with red hair admonished.

Lloyd stepped through the kitchen doorway. He stood beside his mother, his hands on hips. "Trouble, mom?" He leaned forward slightly. His six-foot frame carried two hundred pounds of hard muscle.

"No trouble, son. This young man was just about to leave. Seems he forgot his shoes."

Arnold looked up at the big man filling the doorframe. He was no match for that black giant. "My pa will own this diner someday, soon. Then we'll see who will be leaving." He turned abruptly and stalked out. His face red with anger.

He pushed past Carlos and Mark entering the diner. "Watch out!" Arnold clinched his fist.

Mark winched and cradled his wrist. "You're the jet ski rider."

"That's right, King of the Seven Seas." Arnold grinned and slammed the screen door.

Mark pushed the screen open. Right hand reflex, he groaned in pain. He shouted out. "You're gonna pay, jerk!"

Carlos stopped him. "You're in no shape to fight."

"What kind of trouble is brewing, now? You boys get in here." Martha looked at the bloody scratch on Carlos' arm. She tenderly touched Mark's wrist. He flinched. "You boys have practiced one morning. Do you plan on surviving the summer?"

"Minor setback." Mark's face grimaced.

"Indeed." She probed his wrist with a feather touch. "Nothing out of place."

"This will give Mark time to work on his left hand toss," Carlos said.

"God guides us in mysterious ways. How did you hurt the wrist?" Martha frowned.

"Fell on the jetty, slipped," Mark said.

"He fell because that jerk that just left used his jet ski to shower water on Mark. No accident!" Carlos explained.

"I'll fix an ice pack; come into the kitchen. Paul, give the girls more soda."

In the kitchen Carlos watched the waitress fix a shrimp salad plate. "That will make a good snack before lunch."

Martha shook her head, no. "Your grandfather said to feed you boys. When this diner opened forty-odd years ago the help ate shrimp and sometimes steak. Times change. You might enjoy the deluxe hamburger or today's special, spaghetti with sausage and meat balls."

"Hamburger please, two, I'm big. We had a thin slice of pizza for breakfast," Carlos said.

Once Mark had his wrist wrapped with a bag of ice, Martha cooked the burgers.

Carlos swallowed down two hamburgers, a large order of fries, onion rings, and a large chocolate shake. He dabbed the last fry in ketchup and gulped it down. Carlos smacked his lips. "Delicious! Now I know who cooks the best food in Crescent Bay."

"This diner will lose money with you working here." She watched Carlos clean the plate of the last onion ring. Mark had settled for one hamburger.

"Finished, and the fault of my appetite is your great cooking." Carlos stacked his plate on the dishwashing rack. "And, won't the summer tourist make the diner tons of money."

"With the new resort and take-out chains, the diner is hurting financially. So called Health Code violations were reported anonymously. Your granddad needs money to fix and refurbish." She frowned, etching deep black lines in her forehead.

"The kitchen sparkles. What violation?" Mark surveyed the room. Copper pots and pans hung over the stainless steel worktable. The griddle was sizzling with hot grease. Two large refrigerators reflected light off their clean white surface.

"Complaints, meaningless, to my reasoning. A leak in the plumbing on an outside faucet. The health inspector said we need copper pipes and a new modern dishwasher with scalding heat." The big woman paused breathed deeply, contemplating. "First everything tested okay, rated A. Then they come back, find the leaking faucet. Test the dishwasher again. This time running every hot water spigot while testing the dishwasher. The result was two points below standard. Replace all existing pipe with copper, they ordered."

"Granddad must have money saved." Carlos suggested.

"Yes, and he advanced Lloyd every dime for college. The diner is making money, but not fast enough to pay for the health department's sudden demands. Your granddad could borrow, but he would have to mortgage his home. I'm afraid he's stuck up the creek without a paddle. He's seriously considering selling the diner. Retiring completely."

Paul took plates from the bus tray and sprayed them with the rinse hose. "Doesn't seem fair. My hands are pink from this scalding water." Steam rose around his face.

The big lady put her arm around Mark's shoulder. "That young Arnold boy has a mean streak. He needs to learn a lesson. People shouldn't make trouble for nobody on purpose. Not right. Best way is to make another's life more easy, not more difficult. You stay away from him, my advice."

Mark nodded.

"End of your shift in one hour. You go home now, Paul. Cool down. Take a swim in the surf." Carlos put on a rubber apron.

"You take off. I'll start my shift early." He looked out the door at the two girls at the counter.

Carlos slapped Mark on his left shoulder. "I have an idea, beach camping. It would be rugged, good conditioning. Sleeping bags under the stars."

"At the state campground, of course." His friend would have them sleep on white-hot charcoals to meet girls.

Carlos grinned and went to work. First task, deliver clean napkins to the girls at the counter.

CHAPTER FIVE

Peeping Tom

PAUL MADE A quick stop at the bungalow to don baggy shorts and pick up the weirdly painted boogie board. Graffiti art wasn't his only passion. He loved the beach on the summer weekends like any native Californian.

He walked along the edge of the cliff searching for a path down to the beach. He was about to give-up when a bicycle rider came around the bungalow and headed toward him. Maybe the local knew a short cut to the beach. Paul waved.

The man on the bike lifted his cap and waved. Paul recognized his granddad.

"I saw you from the diner and figured you were searching for a path to the beach. Got a boogie board, I see."

"It was in the bungalow. It's okay?"

"Sure, you take whatever you find, enjoy. I can save you a long walk to the road leading to the pier. See that boulder just ahead. The one marked with graffiti? That boulder marks the path down to the beach. I used the path many a time when your grandma was alive and I was younger. I jogged from the house on the hill to the diner, sometimes on down the path and then I'd swim a few miles. Now, I ride the bike to the diner in the afternoon, everyday. Hate to compromise exercise, but being past seventy slows a man down some. You'll find out someday."

"Thank you for pointing the way." Paul stopped beside the rock. His granddad was staring at the layers of graffiti covering the boulder. "And thank you for giving me a job at the diner. I guess you know about the trouble back home."

"I was in trouble once for doing a stupid thing; I was about Mark's age. I drank beer with a friend. We took a car for a joy ride. I realized what responsibility meant when my dad saw me in that jail cell. I'll never forget the shame I felt. We learn from our mistakes."

"I won't cause any problems. Honest." Paul edged around the boulder.

"Well, don't punish yourself. From what I hear you're lucky to be alive. Maybe you'll do something with your life. You've been given a second chance. Be careful going down, the path is steep and the sand shifts underfoot."

"I'll be real careful. I'll see you later, grandpa."

"Have fun." He turned his bicycle and headed back toward the diner.

The climb down to the beach on the switch-backed trail was slow. Paul gripped the boggie board. Rocks and shale and sand broke free and skittered before his feet.

As he neared the base of the cliff, thundering waves crashed louder and louder, pounding the beach. The tide was out. This stretch of beach disappeared when the tide was full. The waves cut gorges and fissures along the cliff. Stunted trees and brush clung to the face of the cliff.

He was near the bottom, breathing deeply. The path rounded a clump of brush and rocks shoulder high. A kitten scampered from under a large shade rock and a girl shrieked. "Peeping Tom!" She flattened herself on the beach towel and snapped the back of her halter.

"Sorry, I didn't see you." Paul wished he had been more attentive. She was beautiful.

"You were looking, you're not blind." She stopped her tirade, seeing the hurt look on his face, his hunched shoulders. "Perhaps you're innocent, but I doubt it." She stood up.

Paul guessed that she was slightly taller than him. He lifted his heels and rose on his toes gaining an inch in height. Her body carried a little extra weight, she was probably heavier than him. Her curves and her breasts, that he honestly didn't see naked, were perfect. She was very beautiful. Paul felt his heart quicken a beat.

She adjusted her halter-top, pulling the straps tight. The stripes, blue and white, didn't match her polka-dotted shorts, red and yellow. Her black hair curled gently, neck length. A cameo face, with big moon eyes black and shinning. Her chin stuck out defiantly.

Paul finally found his voice. "I'm not a peeping Tom. I am innocent. I just came down to ride the waves." Paul glared at her a long moment.

She stared back, a silent stand-off.

After a long awkward moment of staring, Paul stepped around her beach towel and walked away.

"Well, okay, go ahead and surf, Mr. Surfer," she finally said and leaned down to pick-up the kitten.

Paul ran down the slight beach incline and hurled himself into the sea. He flopped badly, slapping his chest and chin against the board. He ignored the pain. He paddled furiously, kicking hard, fighting the sea, riding into and through a six-foot wave rolling into shore. He broke free of the surf, gasping for air. The boogie board swiveled toward shore. He lifted his head and searched the sea.

Two surfers in bright orange wetsuits rode waxed surfboards on a thundering wave. The boards skimmed the water, the tail fins cutting a path on the white foam. Expertly they cut free of the wave and paddled out, to wait and hope to ride a bigger wave.

Paul judged the waves rolling in and waited. He watched a fisherman in a red baseball cap and red beach shorts raise a twenty-foot fishing rod over his shoulder. The fisherman whipped the rod outward, line whirled off the reel, sending the bullet sinker over the surface of the green water.

Paul kicked the water, turned slightly. The girl on the beach was standing before an easel, looking directly toward him. He slapped the water. "Who's a peeping Tom?" A wave lifted him high, he kicked, but the wave passed.

A jet ski raced along the surf, accelerated, zigzagged, cutting the surf line. A surfer lost balance, a wipe-out in the wake of the jet ski. A pair of bottlenose dolphins dove for deep water.

He rode the swell and turned his attention back to the girl. She was one of the top ten prettiest girls he had ever seen in his life. A knock-out, and out of his league. He was shorter than her. Two clusters of pimples were living on his cheeks. His lips were kind of puffy. His body was tapered, slightly pudgy, although he wasn't really fat. No point in dreaming. She was definitely out of his league. Paul caught a six-foot wave, cut left, riding the crest, into the tube, finally kicking out.

He wiped-out on the next wave, lost his board, and had to bodysurf to shore. He retrieved his board and decided to leave. He missed his friends. Without his friends, time went slow and fun became boring. Besides, he was tired and hungry. He had reported to work at six and skipped breakfast and lunch.

The girl was holding a canvas and brush. The easel was folded beside the basket. She was probably leaving too, Paul thought. She waved. Paul walked up to her. What now, he wondered?

Connie dabbed paint on the canvas, quick strokes with her tiniest brush, the finishing touches. A little cloud raced over the sun. Her brush whisked over the cloud.

Sometimes she surprised herself by her speed and force. She used furious brushstrokes. Quick, hard, threatening to tear the canvas. Spots of gold paint spattered on the kitten's tail.

She added specks of orange to points surrounding the pink cloud. The solo cloud in the sky was shaped like a heart. A cluster of palm trees shot into the sand like giant arrows. The sun was peeking over the violet edge of the horizon. She stepped back. One last light ray ignited whitecaps into rainbow hues. Now. The balance was right. "Fini!"

Her kitten hissed. Paul jumped back, stepped on a shell, tilted and fell. The board landed on top. The girl giggled.

"My name is Connie. And, my cat is called Castaway. I found her under the pier after a storm. She probably washed overboard off someone's sailboat or a cruise ship or oil tanker. Her history is a mystery. Castaway is the only one that knows."

Paul tentatively extended his fingers to the little ball of orange fur. The kitten sniffed and licked salt from his hand. "Hello, Castaway. My name is Paul."

"What do you do for fun beside surf? As you see, I like to paint."

Paul couldn't tell her about his friends and the forty-foot long by twelve-foot high graffiti art letters on display in the riverbed. Eighty gallons of paint and months of labor went into the project. "I play football with my brother, sometimes. Next year I'll play freshman football, maybe." A big maybe, he was a clumsy ball handler and a slow runner. He carried too many extra hamburger and French fry pounds.

"I'm a freshman now, or is it a freshgirl?" She smiled.

Was she showing superiority or just having conversation? "I guess you finished painting." He struggled to keep her interested, at least for a moment.

"You take the painting. My efforts at three dimensional imagery. See the pattern of horizontal lines then a vertical drop with a close up center object highlighted with color blends—blue mixed with violet. Of course, everything is block framed."

Paul looked at the blue sea and crashing waves in the painting. He knew something about color, design, pattern. The interrelationship of design and color was ringing a bell in his mind. Probably his old art teacher's lecture. "No, this is too beautiful, too much. I can't accept." He lumbered to his feet. The kitten scurried away.

"Only a watercolor, please, take it with my apology." Connie stooped and picked up Castaway.

"No, your work is too beautiful."

"Please, take it and I'm sorry. This is just a study. An experiment, my art teacher advised me to experiment. See the glitter effect. I mix the tiniest amount of fine sand with the paint. My teacher said you learn to paint the canvas, then begin to carve into the canvas, and the great artists like Paul Cezanne, sculpt the canvas." She paused and studied her canvas. "Someday I will be free to paint. Now, every painting is a study of art. The sail, an abstraction of colors. The ocean, power and magnitude. A palm tree, symbolizing serenity. I am searching, studying techniques, exploring styles." Connie stopped, caught her breath, smiled. "I'm sorry. I was rambling on and on about art. I don't even know if you like art, but I suspect you do."

"I love art. But, I'm no artist, like you."

"You painted the football trophy and graphics on the Volkswagen." Connie held the painting in the warm sunshine to dry completely.

"How could you know that?"

"Artists are very observant. And, this is a small community with only one new yellow bug this season. Your trophy exemplifies the still life art. Landscape art, I love. And, of course portraiture. The masters included all three in combination on one canvas. You see in my, your painting, the surfer is the portrait, the sea the landscape, and the blanket with radio and soda on the beach the still life. There I go again, rambling on about art."

"You know a lot about art."

"And, I can recognize talent."

Paul blushed.

A flash of sunlight caught the canvas she held toward him. On the highest wave in the picture, there he was riding the boogie board. "That's me! I'm a model. Wow! Thanks."

Paul took the canvas and admired the seascape. "You live near here?"

"At the resort. Have a soda?" She reached down and pulled a cherry soda from her paint basket. The kitten in the basket licked her palm. "Might be too warm." She handed him the drink, fingers touching.

"Thanks." Paul popped the top and took a long drink. "Tastes cool enough. I live in a bungalow at the top of the cliff near Frank's Diner. Frank's my grandfather."

"Do you like to ride horses?" Connie picked up her easel.

"Dirt bikes." Paul stopped. She was suggesting a future meeting, a date. "I like riding a horse, too."

A huge dog suddenly leaped from behind rocks without a sound. Connie screamed. The kitten jumped out of the basket of paint tubes and brushes and leaped at Connie. Paul stumbled backward. The dog charged him.

Paul shook the soda and sprayed the nose and gapping mouth of the beast. The dog yelped, turned in a complete circle and ran toward Connie.

"Moondoggy, sit. Now, sit!" The big canine growled, but obeyed her command. Connie patted his head. "Good boy, sit."

Big black eyes glared at Paul. The low rumbling growl continued.

"It's okay. The dog won't bite. That's my brother's dog, Moondoggy. My brother named him after some character in an old beach party movie from the 60's. My brother is probably searching for me. He thinks he's the boss when my folks are away."

Moondoggy sat obediently beside Connie. Paul stopped backtracking. How bad could a dog be named Moondoggy.

The dog whined. His long pink tongue lapped cherry soda from his snout. The bright white line of sharp teeth kept Paul at a distance.

"My over zealous brother, my guardian while my parents work. He'll order me home and tell you I'm not allowed boyfriends. My parents must meet everyone I talk too. My brother is possessive. A pain! Please, leave now. He'll only cause trouble." Connie took a deep breath. "We'll meet for riding. Better if I pick you up. Where?"

"Across the street from the diner. The bungalow on the cliff edge. What time?" Paul picked up his board and picture.

"Tomorrow morning, ten. Hurry, my brother is a real jerk. My parent's enforcer. And, my parents are away for the weekend."

"Parents are so illogical." Paul turned and scrambled around the cluster of rocks and up the path. He breathed deeply, looked back and saw a tall boy racing along the shore. Paul recognized the troublemaker at the diner this morning.

Halfway up the cliff, Paul stopped. The boy was standing beside Connie yelling at her and pointing toward the path and Paul. She picked up her towel, basket and kitten and walked away. Her brother followed and continued his screaming. Paul caught a few words. "Trash! Dad will hear. Rules!" The voice faded.

Paul crouched, catching his breath. Just when his luck seemed about to change, whammy! Forget the date. He might as well get use to a doomed summer. Wearily he trudged up the cliff path.

CHAPTER SIX

Hot Springs

MARK CLICKED THE switch on the blender and the ceiling light bulb dimmed. So far they had hooked up a microwave, hot plate, toaster and coffee maker. Pots, pans, plates, forks, knifes and spoons littered the sink area. Every box along the wall containing restaurant paraphernalia was open. Not one box had been removed to the storage shed. The blender stopped.

Paul made a neat bow with his tennis shoelace and stood. He looked out the window and down the cliff path.

"Expecting someone?" Mark opened the lid and smelled the concoction of glacier water, fruit cocktail, wheat germ and cod liver oil.

"Add the eggs," Carlos said.

"No more mixing. Get the mugs, and the eggs, then a toast to health."

"Ugg! You two are nuts. Make up a dream potion for strength and gouge on cold pizza for breakfast. Something wrong with that picture?" Paul rolled his sleeping bag. He was free from work today and wondered about Connie's offer to ride horses. Would she show?

"This can't hurt and it might help." Mark poured the mugs full. "Energy drinks."

Carlos cracked two eggs and dropped one in each mug. "Down the hatch."

Carlos and Mark exchanged looks and gulped down half the glass of yellow goo. Both grimaced. Mark smiled first. "A glass with every meal."

"Impossible!" Carlos gagged. "Perhaps a sprinkle of cinnamon for taste."

"Or chocolate." Mark forced himself to drink more.

"How about cayenne pepper." Paul notched his belt. He pulled a clean white T-shirt over his head. He wore baggy blue shorts, black high top tennis shoes, no socks.

"My wrist feels tingly. Probably helps heal injury."

"Who invented that mess?" Paul moved to the window.

"Yucatec Indians, my ancestors." Carlos gulped and gagged again. "Mayan blood."

Mark emptied his mug. Grimaced.

"Never mind, ask a stupid question?" Paul mumbled. He ignored his brother and searched along the cliff edge. She wasn't coming he thought.

"Carlos is proud of our drink and our dedication. Who made you food critic, anyway?" Mark said. "Remember you're here because you broke the rules, not us."

"Sure, sure, drink your poison. Probably both get sick. I don't care."

"You don't care." Mark frowned. "What do you care about?"

A knock on the door ended the exchange. "I got it." Paul scrambled past the table. He opened the door.

"Ready to go riding?" Connie smiled.

Mark and Carlos gawked at the girl in the doorway. She waved. "Hello."

"My brother and his friend." Paul pointed.

Connie nodded to the boys and stared past them at the painting on the wall. "Wow! That picture is awesome."

"You like art, you should see some of the street art near our home." Mark winked at Carlos.

"Right, big art. Big, big art." Carlos stretched his arms out wide.

"Come on! They want to joke about art." Paul blocked her view of the painting. He pulled the door closed.

"We love art!" His brother yelled and Carlos laughed.

"Don't pay any attention to the two clowns. I admire street art, just like you admire that weird painting on the wall."

"I have seen thousands of paintings in books and museums. There was something about that painting. Something familiar. I recognize the art, impressionism, but I can't recall the artist. Who painted the wild seascape?"

"My grandpa said she was a struggling artist." Paul lengthened his stride to match her longer steps. "I looked for a signature. Nothing. I think the artist left before finishing the painting. Patches of canvas are visible in the sky and sea."

"The mystery artist. Beautiful flow of colors, abstract design. Makes me think of the Spanish artist, Joan Miró. Master abstractionist. He painted what he saw in his dreams." Connie clapped her hands. "I recognize the artist style from somewhere, a museum collection, art exhibit, magazine, somewhere? The name will come to me. Something will jolt my memory. A word clue, a dream . . ." She frowned with concentration. "Right now I'm drawing a blank."

Paul grinned. "The painting looks like pools of ink poured over a sunset."

"Poetic description. You like art. Your brother and his friend were right." Connie turned off the brick path and Paul followed.

The horses were tied to the fence post around the side of the bungalow. The couple mounted and rode north along the cliff edge. Connie said, "we ride a mile and then we move into the hills above Crescent Bay."

"Lead the way." Paul gripped the saddle horn with his left hand. He held the reins, but the horse followed without guidance from him. He was grateful for that; he didn't know much about horses. The ride was easy, so far. They followed a path alongside the road to the pier. Connie turned away from the pier and they rode north a mile on the beach along the edge of the towering cliff.

Connie directed the horse into a narrow gorge leading away from the cliff edge. The big animals plodded up the steep trail. A cloud passed over and the shade cooled riders and horses momentarily.

"A storm is coming in tonight." A sudden cold blast of air made Connie shiver.

The horses passed a ring of rocks for a campfire. The wind whistled. The eerie sound echoed in hollow caves and crevices cut into rocky ridges and canyon walls.

The trail narrowed, Paul's horse fell behind. He bounced and bobbed, his thighs chafed. Connie moved rhythmically with her mount. Graceful motion, she knew how to ride.

Rolling hills cut by deep arroyos. Rock outcroppings, huge boulders and ragged ledges marred the placid curves of hill and meadow. On the hills, groves of avocado and orange trees were surrounded by wild brush and scrub oaks. Grapevines crisscrossed the landscape. Picturesque farmhouses and red barns were locked in with fence posts. Far on the eastern horizon rose the jagged peaks of the Sierra Nevada Mountains.

"How much further is the mineral bath?" Paul yelled.

"See the Indian hieroglyphics on the face of that huge rock ahead?" Connie pointed. "Just beyond is the mineral spring."

"You're sure? I'm lost." Paul admitted.

A rabbit bounded across the trail spooking Connie's horse. The mare kicked hoofs in the air, jumped sideways. "Easy, easy, gentle lady." Connie's soothing voice calmed the animal.

Connie reined her horse, stopping on the flat rocky ground near a sheer cliff edge. "I've painted this scene."

Paul's horse halted beside Connie's horse. His horse shimmied sideways, closer to the cliff edge. If animals can sense fear this horse should read his emotions in the Panic Zone. He peered over the edge. His whole body was shaking. The horse shied away from the drop off. Thank you, God, Paul prayed.

Far below the surfers looked like ants on a sugar roll. On the horizon a sailboat skipped and danced over the waves. Far to the north a fog bank slowly retreated from the hills out to sea. A red tailed hawk sailed along the face of the cliff.

"My family spends every summer here. Well, they used to spend every summer at Crescent Bay. My father was a sailor and met my mother, a waitress, when he was stationed in San Diego. They fell in love, married, achieved great business success, and raised two children. My father is wealthy and works day and night all year without vacation." Connie patted the neck of her skittish mount.

"It was not always that way. We used to camp in a tent on the beach in the state park south of Crescent Bay. And, we were so happy. More money equals more work. Father bought a resort condominium. No more tent camping. Now, I seldom see my father or mother. The restaurant business takes all their time." Connie's gaze shifted from the sea to Paul's face.

"My dad works at the post office. He plays golf with his friends. We seldom talk. I guess our relationship is a toss-up. He's busy doing his thing. I'm busy with school and friends I hang-out with."

"We have something in common, common parents." Connie laughed.

Paul grinned. "I'll bet my parents are more strict."

"Wanna bet!"

The two exchanged consoling looks and both smiled.

Connie pointed toward the pier. "Watch for news helicopters when the storm hits. Every time a storm threatens, the reporters stake out the old pier as a likely disaster to happen. Unfortunately, the tide will be at the highest surge when the storm hits tonight. Hurricane Jorge is raging below the Baja Peninsula. But, the reinforced pilings should save the pier." Connie blushed. "I'm no expert on weather. I read the high and low tide sign on the lifeguard station; the sign gives a weather forecast."

She guided her horse away from the cliff edge, Paul's horse followed. They passed a series of giant rocks lining the trail. Spray painted messages crisscrossed the rock.

"Dammit! Can't people leave things the way they found them. Taggers will destroy the ancient Indian symbols next. What gives anybody the right to destroy public land or anyone's land, anywhere?"

Paul didn't answer. He was guilty of the same crime.

The horses passed the last rock, blue and red paint smeared. Water flowed down a high ledge bubbling and steaming. A large pool was cut into the rock. Thick moss and ferns laced the edge of the pool. Hot vapors swirled above the mineral water. Bubbles, like strings of pearls, circled the rocks near the exit of the pool. Branches from an aged ironwood tree shaded the pool. A giant pine beside the pool looked like a corkscrew aimed at the sun.

The water tumbled over a rocky ledge into the pool. Steam hovered above the crystal clear water. A cluster of pussy willows sprouted between a rock and a log. Twin butterflies shared a golden flower. Mirror perfection, orange and black dot symmetry, wings pulsing like heartbeats.

Connie reined her horse in a shaded spot beside the pool. The breeze swept in from the sea, cool and refreshing. She dismounted and removed a packaged lunch from the saddlebags. She had tuna sandwiches, big ripe purple plums, tortilla chips and several cartons of grape juice. She tucked a beach towel under her arm.

Paul dismounted awkwardly. His butt was sore from bouncing on the saddle. His thighs were red and itched from rubbing the flanks of the horse. Gingerly he sat on a log, picked up a stone and skipped it across the pool.

Connie dropped a beach towel beside him and set the food on top. A squirrel scampered along the limb of an oak tree. Perched on the stump of a tree trunk, two blue jays squawked alarm and examined the couple. The horses ignored the locals and buried noses into the water, drinking deeply. The beige mare snorted disapproval, preferring colder water. The pair nibbled the rich grass and clover lining the pool, content with the morning snack.

"Should I tie the horses to the tree?" Paul stretched his aching legs.

"No, they know me and this place. They love to graze beside the pool. There are two more pools higher up, but this is the largest. The Indians believed the water stops pain and heals wounds."

Connie slipped off her boots and tentatively tested the water with her toes. "Like bath water." She splashed a handful of water on Paul. "Hot stuff."

"This hideaway is worth the steep climb." Paul surveyed the landscape. They were in a narrow cleft in the rugged hills. From this height the shoreline stretched to distant horizons, a narrow white band of breakers rippled in the sunlight. Pacific Coast Highway ran alongside the cliff edge. A line of palm trees waved from a rocky ledge a thousand feet below.

A harvest of new blossoms covered the hillside. A California eruption of summer flowers. Petals of purple, yellow, gold and orange mixed with whites and blues. A delicate lace of flowers shimmering in the light breeze.

"Look how fast the clouds move. Isn't it awesome?" Connie was staring into the pool watching the patches of whiteness slip across the water. "I love motion. I love to paint clouds flying across the sky, whitecaps, palms swaying, sailboats racing to a safe harbor. The motions of mother nature when she's angry. And, her rainbow after."

"And horses, I'll bet." Paul looked up. Big smoky clouds rambled across the sky. The clouds expanded and swirled, creating skeleton bones stretching across the blue. Sunlight cast golden rays between shifting white fragments.

"The clouds are like giants entering the arena to engage in battle. There's a storm brewing. I love to paint outdoors. I sometimes paint at night when there's a moon. The stars, phosphorescent waves crashing. Motion, capturing the midnight motion." Connie kicked her feet and sent ripples across the pool. "You're a good listener."

"Thanks." Paul flicked a pebble into the pool.

Ferns stretched delicate fingers directed by gusts of wind echoing through the canyon. A robin perched on an oak branch extended over the pool. The bird's eyes glinted in the sunlight. In the pool the image of the robin's red breast merged with the golden sand. Connie stared at the image. "And I love to paint water, like the French impressionist painter Claude Monet. Refraction, the colossal imprint, deep intricate patterns in motion." Connie took a deep breath.

Paul stretched and watched the huge clouds floating past.

"The storm is scheduled to hit after sunset. But, the day is beautiful." Connie kicked her feet again distorting the clouds lumped together on the pool's mirror surface.

The treetops swayed in the gentle breeze. A spider web of shadows and sunrays reflected in the pool, bent by the current and Connie's splash.

"Do you ever think about tomorrow, Paul? What your future will be?"

"I suppose I'll work, marry a beautiful girl like you, buy a house and car and raise children." Paul gulped and thought, married with children. "A fine car, fast, maybe a Mustang 5.0."

"I want a sports car." She laughed. "A red sports car."

"I'm saving for a car." Paul had two hundred dollars in the bank. He couldn't buy the tires for his dream car.

"What kind of work?"

"Hey, you want to know everything about me. I will work and be happy at whatever I do. And, I'll make a fistful of money." Paul hesitated, he didn't know his future job. Paul turned and looked at her. "I haven't decided. Maybe a cop." He answered without thinking and wondered why he said cop.

Paul turned away and looked in the pool. She looked serious. He felt stupid. He wasn't going to be a policeman, no way. He said it to impress her. "And, I've thought of joining the Marine Corps," he added lamely. Why not, he was already a fool.

"The police protect and serve, a noble cause. I've thought of joining the Navy. See the world. I would keep sketch books of all the sights." She frowned. "But, I think you should join to serve the country, not paint the world."

"My turn to ask a question? What kind of sport car will you buy?" Paul felt safer talking about cars.

"The Porsche is hot. I'll have money, because of my famous Surfer Painting, inspired by you. So, I can afford the best. How about the Ferrari?" Connie smiled. "The Corvette is snazzy. In a lifetime I might own all three. My goal is to live past 100 years and see my grandchild become President of the United States."

"Why not yourself. President Connie! I'll vote for you. First woman president of America."

"Perhaps, but I'd rather be an artist. More romantic."

She kicked the water again and then sank her toes into the sand. Suddenly, she yelled in pain.

Paul tensed, looked around for a bear or another wild dog. "What's wrong?"

"A sticker or something in my heel." She lifted her leg and bent the foot toward him. Paul rested her foot on his knee. He peered closely. A tiny trickle of blood seeped from her skin. A splinter of glass sparkled in the sunlight. "A piece of green glass. Don't move."

Using his fingers like tweezers, his nails pinched the glass splinter. He held her ankle firmly. Gently he extracted a tiny fragment of glass.

Connie gasped. "It hurts." A tear rolled down her cheek.

"You're brave."

"My ancestors were tough. My father's name, Swanson, he's Swedish. A lifeline of explorers, adventurers and soldiers. My mother's ancestry can be traced to the Conquistadors. Ancient Aztec blood flowed in her veins."

"I have Italian and Irish mixture." He laughed. "Our ancestors together cover Europe."

"And the culture of ancient Mexico," Connie added.

Paul dipped her foot in the mineral water and washed the wound.

"Look, you can see pieces of a broken bottle. Why are people so senseless? Probably a weekend cowboy killing a pop bottle. Shooting guns scares me to death."

Paul knelt by the edge of the pool. Carefully, he picked a dozen pieces of green glass from the bottom. "Some people don't care about beauty or wildlife. Feel better?"

She swirled her foot in the water. Her face reflected beside his in the sunlit ripples. He was looking at her. She turned her head. They kissed.

He never thought about being in love before. This was a strange and new feeling. A feeling beyond his experience. She made him feel dizzy. Love, he couldn't explain, the sudden overwhelming desire to impress her.

A motorbike roared up the trail. Abruptly their lips parted. The bike raced into view. Connie jumped up. "Quick, hide. It's Arnold, my brother."

The bike skidded to a halt. "This isn't a state park, this is no man's land. I carry a gun for snakes. And, I see a snake." Arnold slid a gun from his jacket pocket. He grinned maliciously.

"Oh please, brother. Don't be stupid. This isn't real. Where did you get a gun?"

He waved the gun. "I have friends. Guns are for protection. Don't worry, I won't shoot your boyfriend." He fired three quick shots into the ravine. The horses whinnied, trampled hoofs, bolted and fled. Paul leaped to his feet, ran five steps and grabbed for the reins, but was too late.

"Looks like you have to walk back down the trail No sense my sister walking. Hop on the back of my dirt bike, little sister."

"I'm having a picnic with my friend. You can turn around and go away. We'll hike back on foot."

"Do it, Connie. It's a long way back. No point in causing pain or trouble." Paul watched the gun Arnold causally sighted at a squirrel screaming alarm.

"Listen to him." Arnold pointed the gun at Paul. He clicked the hammer back. "Bang!" He laughed and said it again, louder. "Bang!"

"You're not funny, brother, you're crazy. Point that gun away."

"You ride back, now. While dad and mom are away on business they depend on me for your welfare. Do I need to inform our parents about your escapade?"

"Oh, you're in charge."

"You are underage. You are going home. Mom and dad know nothing of what's his name. And, I'm sure they would be upset with you running off with a stranger, especially one with a criminal record."

"What are you talking about?" Connie looked at Paul. His eyes looked away.

"I heard some talk about why he's here. He's in trouble with the law."

"You're crazy. Paul wants to be a policeman."

"It's okay, Connie. I'll walk."

"Get on the bike. We're going home, now." He waved the gun wildly.

"Okay, okay, I'll go. Point the gun away."

Arnold lowered the gun. Connie gathered the towel, slipped on her boots, and climbed on the back of the bike. Arnold kicked the starter, gunned the throttle. "Stay away from my sister," he yelled. "I see you again with my sister, I will shoot you."

Arnold pointed the gun above Paul's head and pulled the trigger. The gunshot echoed off canyon walls behind Paul. Paul's face turned white. He stepped back, splashed into the pool. A splinter of glass jabbed his toe.

Connie screamed.

"Relax, it's not a real gun, just a starter pistol. Shoots blanks." Arnold laughed loudly.

"I don't believe you."

"I'll be okay. Connie, do what he says." Paul hobbled on one foot.

"Meet me at the diner tonight. He can't keep me from a public place."

"Stay away, garbage boy." Arnold fired the gun again. He kicked the bike into gear. He twisted the throttle, the motor screamed. He released the hand brake; the rear wheel spun furiously. Rock and dirt ripped free and flew twenty feet. A hailstorm of stones was directed at Paul.

Instinctively Paul turned his face. A golf ball size rock smacked his temple. Two sharp stones pelted his bicep and cut the soft flesh of his underarm.

The bike roared away. A splinter of rock struck through his shirtsleeve. Blood trickled from his armpit, down over his ribs, dripping on a bouquet of wildflowers. Paul lifted his arm. A jagged splinter of lava rock protruded from his skin. Gingerly, he pinched hold of the rock, wiggled, and pulled. The sliver of rock popped out like the point of a dagger. He sat on the ground feeling dizzy.

Blood oozed down his arm and dripped between his fingers. The pain was searing. He dipped water with his cupped hand and washed the blood away. Hope the Indians were right about magical cures, Paul thought.

He wrapped a torn strip of his T-shirt around and around his shoulder, tightly around the jagged tear in his flesh. He relaxed and leaned against a moss covered rock. He looked down the trail, a long hike back. He closed his eyes. Rest, just for a moment, he thought. He could see her face in his mind's eye. Was that love? And he remembered her eyes. He moved and groaned. Blood seeped through the bandage. His head throbbed. Resting his back against a log, he continued to see Connie, for a moment before his mind blanked out.

⛵ CHAPTER SEVEN

The Jetty

AT RECKLESS SPEED the motorbike raced down the trail and along the shore to the resort. They passed the horses running toward the resort's stable. Connie was furious. She remembered the boy last summer, camping with his family; he was terrorized by her brother. Why? Because they surfed together? Now, the same treatment of her new friend, all over again. Her hands gripped the seat; she refused to grab hold of her brother.

Connie explained to her mom and dad about Arnold's overprotective attitude. They listened. Then, they explained that her brother was in charge. When her parents were absent, Arnold was the legal adult with authority she will respect. And, they insisted they must meet any boy she wanted to date. Meet when? Her parents were never around.

The dirt bike came to a stop. Connie jumped off and ran into the house, up the stairs to her room, slammed and locked the door.

Castaway, startled, rolled off her pillow. "I won't cry, Castaway. I'm too angry." The kitten stared at her, a concerned look.

She was going to get even, somehow. She would get even when her parents came to the resort on the weekend. She would tell about the gun. Pacing beside her bed, she felt like a caged animal. She had to get out. She had to meet Paul at the diner. How could she get out, get past Arnold?

She looked out her bedroom window. Connie watched her brother march from the garage to the front porch. His back straight, eyes locked ahead, defiant, angry. She couldn't figure out her brother's moods. He should be happy, instead of vulgar and conceited. He was handsome and smart, attending college. He had friends. Why was he such a monster sometimes? Why did he have to act reckless and dangerous and stupid?

Giant clouds rolled over the ocean horizon. A dark mass of clouds formed a mountain range where sea joined sky. Gray and black clouds crowded together. Blue space was slowly blotting out by the clouds. She would capture the storm's onslaught on canvas. "I'm not staying locked in my room. I've done nothing wrong." Her rebellious voice caused the kitten to respond.

Castaway whined and pawed the bedcover.

"Castaway, I'm going to paint the approaching storm. You stay here."

Sad green eyes objected. The kitten mewed and jumped into the art basket on the foot of the bed filled with paints and brushes.

"Okay, a piece of my palette paper will cover you if it starts raining. And, I'm sure we'll be safe and warm at the diner visiting with Paul before the rain begins. Keep that our secret."

She covered her watercolor pad with a plastic bag, taking her time. She was stalling, waiting for her brother to leave. Hoping he'd leave. He didn't. She could hear the television downstairs.

Arnold guarded her like a prisoner. She collected her art supplies, left her room and hurried down the stairs.

"I'm going to paint on the jetty."

"Better not! A storm is coming."

"I know. I want to paint the storm clouds. You could pick me up on your jet ski in a couple of hours."

"I'll make sure you're there. I can check with the telescope. I'll pick you up if I'm not busy." Arnold clicked the television channel remote control pausing on every sports station.

Connie smiled politely. She would be watched.

"You spend too damn much time painting." He clicked from tennis to baseball.

"Someone in the family is ambitious."

"I'm studying to be a lawyer." Click, back to tennis.

Connie kept silent. Her brother carried only six units last semester. His ambition was to party. Drinking a beer, her brother slouched in the leather recliner.

"Father would disapprove of the beer."

"Father treats me like a man. I like beer. So what! It's my concern. Just like you're my concern." He clicked the remote repeatedly, finally stopping to view a golf shot.

Arnold rambled on for a minute about responsibility and maturity. He always talked more when drinking beer. Connie listened, he was slurring his words.

"And remember, no boyfriend from the kitchen."

Connie glared at him. "You have changed Mr. Big Shot. You forget your days in the kitchen. Proud to help mom and dad run their first restaurant. Now, they own five restaurants and a winery. Dad owns half this resort. Look back, brother. Remember how it was when you scrubbed tables and dumped garbage."

Arnold's mouth opened. Connie whirled around, pushed open the front door and walked out.

"Stay away from him," Arnold screamed. "You'll be sorry. He'll be sorry."

Connie ran down the path. The roar of the surf drowned out the sound of her brother's harangue. She hurried along the shore toward the jetty.

The rock tower supporting the ship's warning light was connected to the shore by a narrow band of rocks. The path to the rock tower was three feet above the tide level. Tonight the high storm waves might drench the surface of the rocks. The end of the jetty was one of Connie's favorite spots to paint. The light marking the entrance to Crescent Bay burned brightly, revolving slowly.

A news helicopter whirred overhead and flew over the old pier. Look for the worst; hope for the best. She remembered the slogan of the reporter, learned in her journalism class elective.

Every time a big storm appeared, like clockwork, the reporters watched the pier. The word was out, the pier was long over-do to collapse. She hoped the old pier would survive. The helicopter continued south, searching for a disaster.

Connie hurried along the path, down to the beach. Waves lashed the shore. Her face glowed, cheeks blushing brightly. Wild and free, she thought, like a storm.

Gingerly she stepped up on the rocks and carefully stepped from rock to rock. The rocks were wet from spray. She took her time and studied her next step before taking it. The wind increased slightly, cooling the trapped heat of the day.

She reached the rock platform supporting the light tower. Settling on the largest flat rock near the tide line, she took the sketchpad from her basket. Castaway blinked green eyes at the sun and went back to sleep. Selecting a yellow China marker, Connie peeled a loop of binding free of the point. She paused and scanned the horizon.

Connie watched the clouds, puffballs dotting the sky, chasing one another across the sea, over the hills and valleys to the mountains. Her challenge, to capture the majesty and poetry of clouds on canvas.

A wave crashed against the rocks spraying the air with mist. Castaway growled uncomfortably and curled into a tighter ball in the basket.

Connie studied her sketchpad. "Storm Clouds at Sunset, good title?" She wrote the title in the margin of the canvas. She used the margin as a notepad for her thoughts. Often she dabbed colors together along the canvas border to study the mix.

Castaway peered over the edge of the basket at the raising sea.

"Don't worry, Castaway. The storm is set to hit after sunset. The sea storm may come early, but we have a couple hours, easy." She winked at the kitten. "Don't Worry! Be Happy!" Connie sang the old song. The wind whipped the words out to sea.

The sun continued moving slowly toward the horizon, the moon close behind. Thicker clouds raced past, covering the sunlight for moments at a time. Patches of blue tried to break through and keep order between the battling cloud giants. Blue notes, a sweet melody lost in the thundering collisions.

Connie shivered. She should have brought a jacket. Her calico shirt rippled from the on shore breeze. The air was cool, soon to be cold. "We'll leave in one hour. And, stop by the diner. Maybe see Paul. And, buy some fish sticks"

Castaway remained curled in a silent ball, refusing to respond to the temptation of fish sticks. A cold drop of seawater landed on the kitten's pink nose.

"Nothing like realism in art. Salt spray mixed with acrylics. I'll leave a patch of canvas bare; a technique made famous by the French painter Henri Matisse. I'll leave a salty patch of empty canvas."

She flicked a speck of paint on her palette. Smeared the blue with the gray and continued to shape the cluster of clouds in the corner of the canvas. "Almost finished. Just a touch more violet."

Connie focused her eyes on the sun racing to reach the edge of the sea. Magnificent, she thought. Artists struggle to express the power and beauty of the sunset. Connie meticulously dabbed a series of pink highlights to the violet horizon, half the sun dazzlingly bright, half a disc in a pool of milky blue sea. A wind surfer, racing with the wind, flew into Crescent Bay. More gray, she decided. She turned toward her basket.

The tide was higher, the water gently rocking Castaway between the rocks. Connie looked toward shore. Half the jetty was splashed with a churning sea. "Looks like we're going to get wet. Sorry Castaway. I'm going to get wet. I'll carry you ashore above my head. We can make it; I'll be careful. Too bad my brother never shows up when I need him."

Connie quickly tucked the canvas in a wrap. She gripped the basket holding Castaway. She hopped across two large rocks before the first hurricane wave hit the rocks below her, flinging tons of water into the air. The rock she stood on was swept with a surge of frothy water. Connie teetered, crouched, barely maintaining her balance.

The wave washed over the jetty. Gingerly, Connie stood erect and took a hesitant step. It was a long way to shore, storm waves battered the jetty. Carefully she backtracked to the higher rocks supporting the light beacon.

A giant wave crashed and swept over the rocks leading to shore. No escape. Could she wait until the tide recedes? High tide was hours away. This was just a freak set of high waves, probably generated by Jorge, the Baja hurricane. She searched her mind for an answer, a way to escape. Wait on high ground. Connie retreated to the base of the tower. She huddled against cold wet stone. The light flashed alarm.

She shivered, the wind turned cold. She clutched the basket. Carefully she tied a long ribbon around Castaway and secured the ribbon to the handle of the basket. There could be a lull in the storm waves, a calm. She could make a dash to safety. Her brother could come. Fat chance!

Connie held the basket close, trying to shield Castaway from the windswept spray. Paul would be waiting for her at the diner. Her stomach growled. Castaway curled into a tight wet ball of fur, mewling misery.

CHAPTER EIGHT

Drowning

Thunder woke Paul. The mineral pool was in dark shadows, the sun fallen below canyon walls. The wind whispered a warning. The storm was near. He said a silent prayer. Paul stood, stretched and focused his eyes on the path. Time to hike home.

He ran down the path at a frantic rate, fearful of the storm and approaching darkness. The trail was easy to follow; hoof prints and tire tracks marked the way. However, in the dark he could easily walk off the edge of a cliff. And, the day was near the end. He kept running and running, struggling to keep his balance.

He became tired quickly. He was dizzy and his head throbbed. Blood seeped from his cut arm. His toe felt like a needle was stuck under the nail. He slowed and ate part of the picnic lunch, the tuna sandwich he pocketed by the mineral pool. He munched a tortilla chip. He was feeling better. Still a little dizzy, maybe just sleepy. He forced himself to keep moving.

Halfway down the trail a thick mist surrounded him and covered the land. The leaves glistened with beads of water shimmering light. Connie would marvel and see a painting in the misty landscape. Where was she now? He shivered. Home safe and warm he thought. It was funny. She was serious about art and trying to be an artist. He was spray painting eighty-foot letters on the concrete wall of the riverbed.

Why? A need to express? Need for identity? Follow the leader? And, her brother. What was his problem? A need for power? Arnold tried to control people, perhaps to cover a weakness. Or a failure. Everyone fails, sometime. We learn from our mistakes. His thoughts tumbled together, confusing.

He broke free of the mist and could see the beach. Paul jogged around a bend, he stopped. This was the cliff edge where Connie stopped the horses and they talked. This time the surf line was without surfers. The waves hammered against the rocks, pounding the beach. He could hear the blare of the foghorn and see the warning light blink on the point of the jetty. A dim cast of lights marked the position of the pier. He could not see the bungalow beyond the bay. He was a long way from home. He continued down the path.

It was close to sunset when he reached the base of the cliff. He stopped to catch his breath. A sand crab burrowed into the sand beside the rock he sat on. Seabirds chattered: panic messages, last minute directions, and stern warnings.

The sky was now filled with clouds. Shadows raced across the face of the cliff. Out to sea the surface was disturbed by scattered bursts of rain. The sun, veiled in white, clung to the horizon. Slowly the sun began the disappearing act.

The surf played a furious melody. Giant waves flogged the cliffs north of the trail to the mineral springs. Rocks twisted lose and vanished in the raging surf. A palm tree, clinging to the cliff, shuttered under the impact of the waves. Storm winds whipped the sand free.

Waves rushed up the narrow stretch of beach in front of Paul, touched the cliff and retreated. There was still a path to the bay. However, the tiny island of sand where Paul stood was shrinking with the approach of high tide.

Crabs scuttled toward the cliff and climbed above the rusty line marking the highest tide. It was impossible for Paul to climb the smooth face of the cliff to safety. He must escape along the narrow stretch of sand along the cliff edge. Combers rolled in and sometimes covered the strip of beach. Thundering storm surf crashed against the rock jetty a mile away.

A mass of black clouds sealed the horizon. The sun was making a desperate effort to shine through the black clouds. The final bright golden streaks of daylight pierced the blackness.

Paul figured there was less than an hour of light left, dim light. No boats, no one walking above the cliff, no help. He made his decision. He would have to race the tide, dash across the patches of foaming surf covering the sand and striking the cliff. He could make it if he hurried. He stood, stretched, and began running along the cliff edge. He ignored the swirling water, only one mile to Crescent Bay. He was racing the tide. He felt trapped, like the comic hero with the walls closing in.

His tennis shoes sank into the soft sand making each step leaden. He stopped and stripped off his shoes, tied the strings and slung them over his shoulder. His feet still sank deeply; he breathed hard. Water washed at his feet.

A surfboard, badly dinged, floundered in the surf. Could be worth salvage, but the weight? Paul thought it could be waterlogged. He examined the sleek board. The fin was sliced in half. He hefted the board. Not waterlogged. A few fiberglass patches and paint will make this board brand new.

Maybe my luck is holding. Worth saving, he decided. The tide raced past and splashed the base of the cliff. The slash under his arm oozed fresh blood. A trickle of blood found a path to his right breast.

He had time. And, he could always use the board if he was trapped by the tide. He hefted the battered surfboard and continued his hike. A series of waves crashed against the cliff ahead of him. His path was blocked. He waited until the waves receded and then rushed forward.

His arm burned with pain. The deep gash was loosely wrapped with the strip torn from his shirt. He needed to stop and tighten the wrap. No time. Before the next set of waves could recede a new set covered the beach and slammed against the cliff. Paul cradled the surfboard and plunged into the shallow surf. He would have to fight the sea. He must paddle around the jetty into the bay. A longer way home. The only way home.

After paddling through the first surf line his white shirt was stained with a pink patch from his blood.

Wave after wave he ducked under, then kicked forward, progressing slowly. Giant waves slammed down, thundering, crushing his chest against the board. Twirling, kicking, grasping, gasping, reaching, breaking the surface. Another wave. Gulp of air, pounding tons of water. Escape, up, kick, kick furiously, up. Air, breath. A last giant crashing wave.

He was exhausted when he broke free of the pounding surf. He rhythmically propelled the surfboard toward the light flashing at the point of the jetty. Waves chopped at the board. He paddled slow and steady.

Paul splashed past a long flat rock jutting from the sea. The first drops of rain fell. Crabs appeared from cave and crevice, lifted claws and caught the raindrops. Paul laughed at the sight of thousands of thirsty crabs. The surging surf sucked him away from the rock.

The wind whistled cold gusts. The black cloudbank moved across the sea, invading the land. The sea raged, whitecaps slapped the surfboard. The light was nearer. Paul quickened his pace. He could make it. Around the jetty into the bay. Waves crashed over the jetty. Patches of thick fog rolled over the mammoth rocks. He spotted a movement near the light, a shadow. Paul stopped and looked carefully, expecting to see a seal.

The wind whipped spray stung his cheeks. The salt burned his eyes. He blinked repeatedly, trying to focus on the light. His eyes were slits, searching to see the light at the end of the jetty. The surfboard rode high on a wave crest. Another hundred yards of wild sea separated him from the light. Someone waved, screaming help.

A flash of lightning outlined the tiny figure. Paul felt the shock of fear jolt his body. "Connie! Connie!" He yelled over and over. He paddled with all his strength toward the light.

Connie clung to a rock, braced against the onslaught of waves. One hour ago the sea was rolling swells, then whitecaps, and now thundering waves, hurricane surf. She should have left. The dark sky and whitecaps had captured her imagination. She had continued painting. Now, she was trapped.

Moments ago, a wave had crashed on the rock tower and swept her canvas away. She almost lost Castaway. The sea was violent; waves crashed over the jetty blocking any escape. She huddled behind the stone tower of the light. She clutched her basket holding Castaway to her chest. Above her the red beacon revolved slowly, warning ships to steer clear.

Wave after wave smashed the rock tower. She was huddled against the stone base supporting the beacon light. She clung with her last strength to a rock that partially blocked the crashing waves.

Paul kicked toward the rock jetty. He was frightened. Any moment she could be carried away by the thundering surf. Paul kicked hard and paddled near the rock wall. Paddling wildly to hold his position, Paul yelled. "Jump, Connie, jump into the trough, between waves. Jump, now!"

"Go for help," Connie screamed.

She had never heard of the rock tower being swept over by waves. Now, huge combers crashed against the rocks sending sheets of water flying into the air. Could she dive into this wild surf? Did she have a choice? Connie stared at Paul struggling in the wild sea. She shifted her position; her leg was cramped. Could she swim in that maelstrom? She massaged her leg cramp and slightly released her grip on the basket handle. A wave exploded against the rocks, water swept over the base and wrenched the basket from her grasp. Castaway was carried away.

A second wave slammed against her legs, carried her over the rocks and into the surging sea. Connie went under. The next wave and the next battered her. She was tossed about like a rag doll in a washing machine.

She kicked and kicked and breached the surface. Paul spotted her, paddled nearer. Her hand, limp and cold, reached for his. Palms met, fingers entwined, gripped. Paul flipped into the water and slid her over the board. She clung to the surfboard. Paul held tightly to the board and kicked away from the rocks.

A set of rolling combers lifted them higher than the jetty. Then, they dipped into a deep trough. They were still near the point of the jetty and Paul felt very weak. Their progress away from the rocky point was impeded by the hammering surf. Sheets of rain swept over them.

Paul was paddling with all his strength. They had to round the point of the jetty or drown. He knew he wouldn't make it. His arms felt like rubber. His legs were numb from the cold. Connie's added weight submerged the surfboard. Water soaked through the chips and cracks of the fiberglass into the Styrofoam.

Connie made feeble efforts to paddle. The white crest of a wave rushed them toward the rocks. Together they thrashed the water with hands and feet. They looked like drowning rats. Paul clung to her legs and the edge of the board. Tons of water raced under them and exploded against the rocks. A riptide pulled them away, out into the dark sea.

The surfboard was sinking. He slipped into the water. The board floated higher. Connie stretched across the board. Her hands barely gripping the edge. Paul's hands clung to her arms. They faced each other. The surfboard thrashed and bucked. Slowly going down.

The two stared into each other's eyes. A wave bucked the board against Connie's chin. "Ouch!" Connie screamed.

Paul's mouth gaped open. "You okay?"

"Bit my lip . . . lip? Libby! The artist is Libby Eden . . ." A wave slapped her face. "Edenstrom!"

"Who?"

"Edenstrom!" Connie shouted. "I told you something would jolt my memory. I remember the painter of the seascape. The impressionist artist, Libby Edenstrom." The wind whipped the name away.

Paul grinned. "You're awesome, Connie."

She kissed him. An icy blue kiss.

CHAPTER NINE

Rescue

PAUL'S SHIFT HAD started at the diner. His brother was late and Mark was angry. Carlos sweet-talked the girls from the state park into a date, pizza and a movie. Pick them up at six, damn, it was past six. He searched the shoreline. Where was Paul? Sneaking around somewhere with his spray can probably, he thought. "Damn!"

Mark stood at the edge of the cliff and looked out at the raging sea. A sprinkle of rain was falling. He scanned the seacoast, empty of people. He saw a lone surfer struggling in the surf alongside the jetty. Who would be crazy enough to surf in this weather? Hurricane surf from the Baja storm, Jorge, pounded the shoreline.

Then he saw the girl clinging to a rock at the tip of the jetty and understood. She was trapped and the surfer was trying to help. God help, the date will have to wait. Mark shrugged. Carlos would have to work overtime.

Two jet skies were above the surf line alongside the pier. Someone must be at the pier to help. He screamed. "Someone drowning! He waved his arms. The wind erased his words.

He turned toward the diner. Cars in the lot, people in the windows. Mark screamed. "Help! Help!" Again and again he screamed. He waved his arms. Was everyone in the diner blind and deaf? Mark turned and sprinted down the path toward the pier.

He broke all records in his downhill race to the pier. The path ended in a steep sixty-degree decent, football field width. Mark bounded down, faltered, caught himself and charged forward. He was panting when he reached the base. He sprinted across the parking lot toward the pier.

He was halfway when his grandfather's jeep roared down the narrow road parallel to Mark.

The horn honked and Mark cut left toward the jeep. His grandfather waited, he held binoculars to his eyes and scanned the jetty. "Hurry son. That girl's in big trouble. And the surfer." The jeep bucked forward and roared across the parking lot. "I saw you waving then race away. I sensed trouble."

A couple of guys chomping hotdogs huddled under the pier beside the jet skis.

Mark jumped from the jeep. "I need your jet ski." He gasped, breathless.

"Screw you, surf rat." Arnold wiped ketchup from his chin.

"There's a surfer drowning out there. And a girl trapped on the jetty." Mark yelled gruffly. "For God's sake help!"

Arnold gulped. "A girl, my sister. Take the ski, follow me." Arnold tossed his hotdog away, grabbed the jet ski and hauled it into the surf. Mark was right behind him.

The sea was black now that the sun was down. Thick clouds blotted out moon and stars. Foaming crests of waves thrashed the jet skis. The riders wobbled, balanced, and maneuvered through the raging sea.

The jets labored against the storm waves, gradually gaining the point of the rock jetty. The beam of the warning beacon lanced out across the blackness.

On the peak of a wave, outlined by the faint glow of the beacon light, Mark saw a surfboard, half submerged. Two people clung to the derelict. He recognized his brother.

Paul stopped paddling. A roaring sound ripped above the howl of the wind. A jet ski bobbed and thrashed the waves, rounding the point. Another followed. Paul kicked hard.

Two jet skis. His brother rounded the jetty first. Followed by Connie's brother.

Paul plunged his arms into the surging water propelling the board over a cresting wave. The pair of skis circled, stopped and floated beside the surfboard.

Paul helped Connie straddle her brother's ski. He climbed aboard behind Mark.

Suddenly a bright light beamed down from above, illuminating the sea. A news helicopter hovered and moved the light toward the rocks, warning the jet ski riders of the danger in the black sea.

The jet ski engines throttled to high power. The skis pulled away from the jetty. The light guided them into the bay and toward the shore.

The jet skis fought the churning sea, bucking and pounding toward the pier. Halfway to shore Connie screamed, "Castaway!"

A familiar basket bobbed on the top of a wave. "Stop!" Paul pounded his fist on Mark's back. "Stop!" He pointed to the basket.

Mark idled the engine and swept alongside the basket. Paul reached out and caught the handle. A wet ball of fur clung to the bottom of the basket. Castaway stared up at him with pitiful eyes.

Moments later the jet skis rested in the shallow surf of the bay alongside the pier. The teens stood on dry sand, safe.

"Dammit, man! You took my sister surf riding in this blast. Freaking stupid." Arnold clinched his fist and drew his arm back. Paul weaved and bumped against Connie.

"Arnold, he saved my life. I was painting on the jetty. Trapped by the hurricane surf. And, you dear brother said you would jet ski me home at five. The time is sunset, past six o'clock. I would have drowned depending on you!"

Arnold looked at his sister a long moment. "Sorry, really sorry."

Connie was shivering. She clung to Paul. "He saved my life."

She felt the warm sticky flow of wetness down her arm. She looked into Paul's eyes. They fluttered.

His skin was chalky. He looked in shock. She felt his body go limp. His eyes closed. He collapsed against her.

She staggered and eased him to the ground. Connie gasped. His T-shirt was red with blood.

The basket slipped from his fingers. The kitten mewed softly and leaped to the sand. Castaway licked the cold fingers of her new friend and hero.

CHAPTER TEN

Beach Party

THE STORM HAD raged all night and half of Friday. Saturday morning the sky was peppered with fluffy cotton clouds. The temperature was rising. By noon the day was perfect.

Paul leaned against the pier rail. He listened while his brother and Connie's brother outlined the boundary of the field and the rules for a football game. The beach party was his granddad's idea. A celebration of the rescue. The football match-up was Carlos' brilliant idea. A friendly game. Mark agreed. Arnold was eager.

Arnold's voice was loud and commanding. "Since you guys are high school age choose one alternate. Call him in to rest someone."

"We don't need favors," Mark said.

"Your brother, the hero, perhaps," Arnold insisted.

"Still wise-cracking, playing the fool. Okay! We'll take Ginger." Mark pointed to the redhead on the ten-speed.

"Who?"

The girls stopped their bikes beside the boys. The tall redhead waved hello. Her blonde girlfriend smiled.

The football debate ended for the moment. All male eyes and thoughts focused on the girls.

Paul waved at the third girl riding a bike. Connie smiled and waved at Paul. She dismounted and took two sodas from the bike's saddlebag. She strolled over to Paul.

Connie pecked his cheek with a kiss. "Hello, Paul." She handed him a soda.

Paul caught her hand and led her away from the group and out on the pier.

"I hooked one! A fish, a fish!" The little girl cranked the reel. She cranked and cranked. Gulls screeched. A pelican looped overhead to investigate. She cranked.

"You caught your first fish!" Her father helped her with the catch. Her mother smiled, proudly.

The couple holding hands walking past, stopped and watched the excitement. The father took a picture of his girl and her fish, a pan size sand bass.

The shoreline was crowded with people. The beach party was in full swing. Hotdogs, hamburgers and chickens sizzled on a dozen barbecues. Picnic tables burdened with potato salad, pasta, fries, chips, dips, pickles, mustard, ketchup, tomato slices, onions and cheese. An assortment of sodas chilled in ice chests. Radios blared three different stations: baseball, hip-hop, and talk. The talk topic, teen dating habits. Where do parents draw the line?

"There's your granddad; did you tell him." Connie beamed a big smile. Frank was fishing further out on the pier.

"I waited for you." He remembered their discussion yesterday after being released from the hospital. Using the internet Connie had verified the identity of the artist of the weird painting in the bungalow. Libby Edenstrom had a web site.

The couple came up to Paul's granddad. He was holding a bamboo fishing rod, gazing absently at the rolling waves. They said hello and began talking rapidly.

The older man leaned against the pier rail, amused by their excitement. He gave everyone off today with pay. Anyway, half the town was at the beach party. He was heartsick. A letter from the health department ordered repairs to start by the end of the month. He would have to close the diner.

The tip of his pole twitched. Quickly, expertly, he released the tie securing his pole to the rail. Once, years ago, a big fish yanked his fishing outfit over the rail and into the sea. Since that day he always made sure his pole was tied down or in his hand. This was only a nibble. He held the pole gently, waiting. After a moment he would check the bait.

He listened half attentively to the two teenagers explaining about art, the painting in the bungalow. Suddenly, his face brightened. He remembered accepting a dozen paintings from the artist they were talking about. The wild colors and abstract shapes didn't appeal to his taste. The collection was stored in the rafters of his garage. If the teens were correct, he owned thousands of dollars worth of art. He felt like dancing a jig. Instead he maintained a stoic appearance, except for the big grin.

Paul continued to talk. "Connie sent an E-mail to Libby Edenstrom."

Connie cut in. "She identified the painting and said her summer at Crescent Bay advanced her art skill tenfold."

"And, she had a swinging time," Paul added. He had read the E-mail.

"She sent her love to you and said she would visit soon. She remembered the painting in the bungalow and said you were very gracious accepting her work to pay the rent."

It was Paul's turn again. "She said she would love to buy the painting back. Any paintings you still have she wants. Nostalgic memories too powerful to express, she said."

"She said to name your price."

"She is very wealthy."

The two teens finished, breathless.

"You two deserve a finder's fee. Maybe ten percent. I'll have to think on this. I have to contact your artist, Libby Edenstrom. The name rings a memory bell. You two run along and have fun."

Paul grinned. His banishment from home was turning up rainbows. He was somewhat of a hero. A news helicopter, checking to see if the pier was possibly doomed by the storm, spotted the boy's rescue and filmed it. The boys were declared heroes on the television news that evening.

In fact his dad was especially pleased. He asked his son to come home. Paul said he was happy working with grandpa. And now, money to burn. And Connie, especially Connie. His luck had turned. Or maybe he had learned to make his own luck.

"We're going to walk to the end of the pier and watch the sunset." Paul grinned.

"Talk about art." Connie took Paul's hand.

Granddad winked. "Sure!" For once he cut the conversation short.

The couple walked further out on the pier. Stopped and looked toward the shore again. Two boys worked with dump truck and bulldozer to build a fort of sand and driftwood. A group of toddlers were busy scooping sand into pails and adding seawater.

A cabin cruiser passed the end of the breakwall, glided gracefully into the bay and dropped anchor. Guests, visiting overnight.

The football players were forming for the game. Words picked up by the breeze floated over the pier. Paul and Connie listened.

"No point taking this game serious. Only point is to help you boys learn to play college style. Course we'll soft pedal." The group, clustered around Arnold, laughed and punched arms. This was going to be easy, Arnold thought.

"You receive and we'll make the center ineligible. To even the sides." Arnold flipped the football hand to hand.

"We have a center," Mark said.

"We call him Rock." Carlos punched Mark's arm.

"And where is Rock?" Arnold looked over the guys from the state beach campground that formed Mark's team. Good thing the game was flag, he thought, tackling would crush the whimps.

"Coming along right now. That big guy running this way. He likes to jog ten miles everyday." Carlos pointed toward the diner.

Mark laughed, remembering yesterday's conversation in the diner. The downcast looks, the hopelessness. "We can't compete against Arnold, his friends play freshman football in college. Our challenge was just plain stupid."

Lloyd offered to help. He revealed his love of football as he flipped three hotcakes onto a platter. He played for his agriculture college; last year they won divisional title. He played tackle.

"Flip for receiving?" Mark offered.

Eyes followed Lloyd as he came up to the boys, grinning. He wasn't even breathing hard.

For the first thirty minutes Arnold's team controlled the ball and scored two touchdowns.

Briefly Mark's team had a chance to move the ball. They fumbled on third down.

Arnold's college jocks moved the ball within field goal range before being stopped. The Rock leaped high and blocked the field goal attempt: a kick aimed to go over the volleyball net, the official goalpost.

Carlos caught the kick-off and ran the ball halfway down field. Arnold was overconfident, sure to be the first team to reach twenty-one. Arnold blitzed past the center. Mark flicked the ball to Carlos. They didn't expect the accuracy with a bum wrist. Switching left handed fooled everyone. But, only once.

The run was perfect. The Rock blocked and Carlos barreled over his equal in size for the score.

"Touchdown!" Mark screamed and did a victory dance. Carlos spiked the ball.

Ten minutes later, within five yards of a final touchdown, Arnold's team fumbled. The ball was recovered by the Rock; he raced for a touchdown to tie the game. The game continued.

Paul and Connie walked out further, hand and hand. Near the end of the pier they stopped again and watched the game. The players looked small, television size at this distance. The action was blurred by the sand raising around the players and the shadows of late afternoon.

Her brother caught a lateral pass and charged the scrimmage line. With uncanny swiftness the Rock shifted left. Arnold bounded into Lloyd's big chest, bounced and landed on his butt.

Lloyd dangled the flag in his face and extended his free hand. Arnold grinned, gripped the hand offered and jumped to his feet.

"Looks like my brother has learned humility," Connie said.

"We all learned from the storm and near disaster." Paul shivered.

They watched in silence for a long moment and remembered. Connie broke the silence. "I thought you would be playing."

"Doctor's orders. Rest and recuperation. Of course, I feel fine. Just tired, like." Paul sipped his soda.

"Looks like the end of the game."

The ball was five yards from the thirty-yard line, fourth down. Rock could possibly muscle the five yards. Maybe not, with three college blockers bunched in front of him. Paul's brother pursed his lips and gave a shrill whistle calling time-out.

Arnold paced the scrimmage line. The score was 21-20, in favor of Arnold's team. His opponents failed extra point was the difference in the score. If they stopped the attack the game was over. The agreed rule was the first to 21 wins if the opponents last chance to tie or exceed the score failed. Mark's left handed hand-off to Carlos and the fumble recovery by Rock kept the score tight, despite the hotshot college players Arnold commanded. The blocked extra point made the difference.

"Look, Paul, Ginger is going into the huddle."

Arnold's team hooted and whistled when Ginger embraced shoulders and leaned into the huddle.

"What the hell's going on?" Arnold yelled a warning. "If she carries the ball, flag her, no stop her, bring her down. Gently!"

The huddle broke. Rock stood back. The line was tight, no receivers.

"She's going to kick," Paul said.

The ball was snapped. Mark caught the snap, set the ball, finger on top, balanced for the kick. Ginger danced, then shot forward.

Two linemen charged past the scrimmage. Rock stood between them and Ginger. They toppled.

Ginger kicked, a karate jab, the technique she used in her soccer games. The ball rose like a rocket, spun and arched over the volleyball net for the score.

Paul and Connie watched the wild hullabaloo on both sides. This time her brother didn't sulk or show anger. He clapped the Rock on the back.

"My brother lost and didn't kick sand in anyone's face."

"Nobody's fighting." Paul grinned.

"Perhaps the hotdogs and soft drinks are too inviting, everyone is scrambling for the barbecue." Connie took a drink of soda.

"No time for dispute. All's well that ends well," Paul said.

"Look, your brother and my brother are jogging together, talking."

"Dedicated to excellence and comradeship. My brother will have your brother thinking of turning pro before college." Connie smiled. "They have something else in common. Both want to be lawyers and both are honest men. Two honest lawyers. The world is changing."

"Look, the girls from the beach camp are joining them."

"Probably for the victory dance. See Carlos, over there, dancing to the salsa music." Paul pointed.

Paul put his arm around Connie and twirled her around. They exchanged smiles, and continued walking toward the end of the pier.

"Perhaps you could show me a sample of your street art." Connie caught his hand and squeezed.

"Art?"

"There is form and excellence in every style of expression."

"Art, you think what I do is art?" Paul frowned, he confessed his crime. "You know? About my graffiti art? Being caught by the police?"

"My brother somehow learned the story. You're a graffiti artist. I guess the crime is painting public property. You still produce art. Look at the painting in the bungalow. In the recent past, no one would buy a painting composite of abstraction and impressionism. Now, Libby Edenstrom's paintings are worth thousands of dollars. Maybe Crescent Bay and my support will turn your art in a different direction."

"Wow! Granddad can sell the paintings, pay off the restaurant debt. No one would pay for spray paint on concrete? And, I guess that's my level of art, low."

"Don't underestimate the value of street art. Rich, expressive colors. Advertisement copies the style. You know something about design. Obviously perspective. Of course, a three dimensional pattern is apparent in most graffiti logos. Someday, who knows where your art will lead?" She paused, squeezed his hand. "And emotion in color." They watched the glowing red sun rolling toward the horizon.

"I think I can understand that idea." He wanted to squeeze back, but his hand was limp and sweaty.

They walked to the end of the pier. They were alone; everyone was on the beach enjoying the party. A bonfire blazed. A boom box blared. Couples danced on the blacktop.

Connie lifted a gun from her back pocket. "Kind of pretty, in a deadly way. My brother gave it to me. He said you told everyone you were cut in the surf on coral on a rock. Arnold told me the truth. He said rock fragments spinning off the bike tire cut you. He said you had a hard head, thank God. He gave me this and said thanks. Will you do the honor?"

Paul hefted the starter pistol. "We learn from our mistakes." He pulled back his arm and flung the gun into the ocean. A loud splash was followed by silence.

A dead calm smoothed the velvet black sea. The only sound the hiss of the tide rushing under the pier. The sun dipped into the sea.

They kissed, a light contact, brief. No words. Holding hands they watched the sunset.

The stars twinkled into view. Gentle waves slapped the pillars. The calm after the storm. The bonfire shot sparks at the golden crescent moon. The storm had washed the sky clear and left a black canvas sprinkled with stardust. The moon smiled.

The rapid thump of paws on wood made Paul turn. The big brute, Moondoggy, lumbered toward him. He could dose the dog with soda again. He grabbed his can balanced on the rail. Moondoggy leaped up and lapped his tongue across the top of the cold drink.

"It seems like he has a taste for cherry soda." Paul tilted the can and Moondoggy lapped the soda.

"I like that brand, myself." Connie put her arm around Paul's back.

The big dog barked and licked Paul's hand with a tongue turned crimson.

Paul raised his cherry pink hand. "Moondoggy the artist," Paul said.

Connie smiled. "That color reminds me of a painting." Connie frowned. "What was the name of that painting? A Picasso painting during his Pink Period. Did you know Picasso had a Pink Period and a Blue Period and a cubist . . ."

END